Redheads need Love: Megan from New Orleans

Dirk Caldwell Romantic Erotic Novels, Volume 10

Dirk Caldwell

Published by Dirk Caldwell, 2023.

This is a work of fiction. Similarities to real people, places, or events are entirely coincidental.

REDHEADS NEED LOVE: MEGAN FROM NEW ORLEANS

First edition. October 16, 2023.

Copyright © 2023 Dirk Caldwell.

ISBN: 979-8223004271

Written by Dirk Caldwell.

Also by Dirk Caldwell

Adventures of Stan
Stan does a Big Girl and gives her a Big Orgasm
Stan Does a Female Police Officer While On Duty
Stan Scores on a Booty Call with Barbara
Stan Takes Barb's Anal Cherry
Stan Teaches Oklahoma Karen About Sex in the City
Stan gets Kinky with Barb on Vacation
Barb Wants more Orgasms with Stan before She gets Engaged to Another Man
Stan Does Barbara's Mom!

Dirk Caldwell Romantic Erotic Novels
A Visit to the Farm with Darla - a Sexy Short Story
A Layover in Omaha with Tina
A Night in Eufaula with Lynn
A Trip to the Lake with Kim
Older Women need Love, too! Erika visits Atlanta
Lessons in Love: Gabriella visits Indianapolis
Big Girls Need Love, too! Barbara from Kokomo
Flight Attendants want Love: Flying High with Jessica
Back to the Farm with Darla - A Sexy Sequel
Redheads need Love: Megan from New Orleans

A Big Girl finds Love: Joann from Shreveport
Lust from London: My Affair with a British Nymphomaniac
Paula's Sexy European Weekend
Mother and Daughter Threesome

Dirk Caldwell Sexy Short Stories
To All the Girls I've Loved Before: Sexy Short Stories Book 1
To All the Girls I've Loved Before: Sexy Short Stories Book 2
To All the Girls I've Loved Before: Sexy Short Stories Book 3

Acknowledgment

Cover image by Racool Studio on Freepik
Back Cover generic airline pilot image by Blake Guidry at unsplash

Introduction

I had only known the very petite, redheaded female Lieutenant Colonel from the Louisiana National Guard only a few hours, but things were going very well. We were naked, facing each other in a hot tub, with my cock buried in her very tight pussy as she straddled me and rode my rigid cock up and down while moaning loudly. I had a finger in her ass, and the other hand was busy caressing her medium boobs for added enjoyment. What made it more fun was that such relations were taboo between an officer, which she was, and an enlisted man, which I was. Let me explain a little.

My name is Dirk. Well, that's not my real name. I'd never be able to have a normal life if I used my real name. I was a single guy just out of the Air Force at the time of this encounter. I enjoyed being unencumbered and the benefits that came from that.

This book is about me and a senior Air Force Officer and gets pretty steamy. Like I said earlier, sexual relationships between officers and enlisted men are taboo, and Megan ends up a very senior officer. The forbidden love aspect of the relationship makes it even more spicy.

As a disclaimer, I always change enough of the information about the ladies so my writing could not possibly be traced back to them. Cities are changed, along with names, occupations, specific characteristics, branches of service for the military, etc. To do otherwise would not be gentlemanly. I do, however, mix in some of my local knowledge about locations. How did I get that information? Let your imagination be your guide. Back to our story.

Friday night at the Officer's Club

I was a single man in Shreveport, Louisiana and at this time in my life was between my service with the Air Force and commercial pilot training. Living with my friend Ronni as a housemate and strictly platonic buddy was saving me money and gave me a friend to hang out with. My days were filled with working on the air base a few times a week part-time as a simulator instructor and trying to sell insurance on other days. I was in a rut, not motivated, with not a lot of money, and was almost depressed. For my social and sex life, I dated several women, none of them seriously. All of them had various levels of needs and desires in the bedroom, and I did my best to keep it all straight.

Ronni worked for the Air Force reserve squadron, and on the weekends called UTA or Unit Training Assembly, she usually wanted me to drive her to the officer's club casual bar on Friday night so she could party it up with the young reserve officers while not risking a career-ending DUI. While I was not eligible to be in that club because I was a retired enlisted man and not an officer, nobody seemed to care when they found out I was Ronni's friend. This UTA Friday, Ronni asked a favor of me while she was getting ready to go to the club.

"Dirk, I have a lady visiting our squadron from the Louisiana National Guard for the weekend. She's a Lieutenant Colonel Squadron Commander, and I want her to have an escort for the weekend. Could you ..."

I grimaced. "Really, Ronni? A retired NCO for an escort? She'll think all the officers were tied up taking care of other visitors. I don't think this is a good idea."

"Now, Dirk ... This is more in the line of an unofficial escort, kind of like someone to take her to dinner and drinks."

"Is she single?"

Ronni saw I was weakening. She smiled and said, "Yes, she's single and not bad looking, either. As a matter of fact, she's cute as shit. C'mon, Dirk! Be a pal and take care of her for the weekend."

I looked astounded. "The weekend? The whole freaking weekend?"

She smiled sweetly. "I seem to recall you grumbling because all your regular gals are not available. Who knows, you might get lucky! She's going to meet us at the casual bar."

She did have a point. Darla and JoAnn were busy or had other plans, and Liz was pissed off at me for some reason. I could use female companionship.

"All right, I'll do it. Let me put a date night shirt on and shave."

She came to me and gave me a sisterly kiss on the cheek. "Thanks, man."

I drove us to the base and on to the officer's club annex, also known as Hangar 2, aka the casual bar. It was located separately from the main club where the Colonels and their ladies enjoyed a dignified drink in quiet surroundings before dining in a room with tablecloths and a uniformed waiter. Hangar 2 on the other hand was more like Animal House. The guys could wear their flight suits or work uniforms and hoot it up away from the disapproving gaze of the senior officers. The casual bar was a lot more fun, and a lot of the officers I knew from my time with the active duty squadron came to the happy hour there on Fridays. I always had someone my age to talk to.

Our usual routine was for Ronni to hang out with the younger officers and get hammered while several of them tried to get in her pants. She usually wanted me to break her out of there if someone got too friendly. I would hang out at the bar and nurse one or two drinks, then Ronni and I would leave for dinner or just go back to the house. Having the lady visitor there would complicate things.

Arriving at Hangar 2, I found a place at the bar with a couple of guys I used to fly with when they were on active duty. Ronni went to join a group of younger guys. After I shot the breeze for about 15 minutes and got caught up with my friends, I noticed Ronni walking toward me with a very petite redhead in tow. This couldn't be ...

"Dirk, this is Lieutenant Colonel Devereaux from New Orleans. Colonel, this is Mr. Dirk Caldwell."

The Colonel stood looking up at me, straight into my eyes. She looked up because she was very petite, under five feet tall, slender, and with dark red hair was a striking visage. Her green eyes looked at me calmly. I extended my hand, which she took.

"Hello, Ma'am."

We shook hands, and the Colonel spoke. "Thanks for escorting me, Dirk. I kept telling Ronni it wasn't necessary. I'm glad to meet you. Please call me Meg."

Meg kept looking into my eyes and held the handshake a few seconds longer than normal. After a moment, Ronni said we could get a table, and all sit together. I said goodbye to my friends and carried my drink to the table that Ronni appropriated. The club was busy and noisy.

Ronni broke the ice. "Dirk recently retired from active duty and is working at the tanker flight simulator on base as a contractor."

Making my social standing clear, "I retired as an E-8, Meg."

She was a bright lady, picking up on that nuance right away. "Since you are retired, there is no issue with us socializing. It's not officer to enlisted fraternization any longer."

I smiled. "I'd hate to get you in trouble with your chain of command."

She smiled back, then looked a bit frazzled, then blushed. With her pale skin and red hair, it was very noticeable. Ronni was watching her intently. She'd seen this before. Some women get flustered when I am around them, it must be due to pheromones or something. Meg was feeling something.

Ronni smiled and said, "I'll leave you two to get acquainted. My table is waving at me, I think they have another round ready."

I smiled at Meg, and she blushed again. "Can I get you a drink?"

She looked relieved. "Oh, yes. That would be great. What are you having?"

"Vodka and club soda."

"I'll get the same."

I waved at the bartender, got his attention, then pointed at my drink, and held two fingers in the air. He nodded, and within a minute we had fresh drinks in front of us.

"Here's to you, Meg." I held my glass up and we clinked glasses in a toast.

She took a healthy pull. "That's good. I was feeling a little ..."

To myself I said, horny? But being a gentleman, I said, "It may be a little warm in here."

We regarded each other openly. Her medium-length dark red hair was styled appropriately for a mid-level officer. She had conservative makeup on, with a gold necklace and pinkish lipstick. She was wearing a nice floral pattern blouse tucked into conservative-length light-colored shorts. She had nice legs, with white sandals and painted toenails. She could not have been over five feet tall. Everything about her was petite. Her face, mouth, hands, fingers, feet, and toes were all tiny. I would guess she would not be over 95 pounds soaking wet. There was an Air Force Academy ring on her right hand, with no other jewelry except a watch.

I broke the silence. "Are you an academy grad?"

She nodded, glad to be on familiar ground. She spoke with a slight southern Louisiana accent, it was charming. "Yes. Class of '80."

I was surprised. "So, you were in the first class that graduated women."

She nodded. "That's right."

I did a calculation. In the service for 13 years. "You're doing very well to be a LtCol already."

She smiled shyly. "I'm a new one. Three women from my class just got promoted to LtCol, I'm one of them. The Louisiana Guard does not have many academy grads, and I kept getting great jobs and doing well at them."

"What brings you to our quaint air base?"

"Some of my squadron members are here getting training from Ronni's group, so I tagged along to see what it's all about. We start training tomorrow, and I'm also shadowing their Wing Commander for leadership mentoring. So, I have tonight free."

I looked at her without comment, and she blushed again. "I don't know why I said it like that, I meant we start tomorrow."

I gently said, "Meg? Am I making you uncomfortable?"

She shook her head emphatically. "No. I mean yes. I can't explain it, I feel like a schoolgirl meeting someone she has a crush on."

I decided to be bold and cut through the bullshit. "Meg, I think I know what it is. Can I take your hand, please?"

She hesitated, then extended a hand across the table. I took it in one hand, then put the other on top of it while looking into her pretty green eyes. She looked straight back at me. Her hand was warm and dry at first, then became moist. She looked a bit panicky.

"How are you doing, Meg?"

She smiled nervously and blushed again. "Okay. Your hand feels ... nice."

I smiled reassuringly. "Are there any members of your squadron here?"

She looked around. "No, I don't think so. Why?"

I tried to look harmless. "So, Ronni and I are the only ones here that know you. Right?"

She nodded, not sure where this was going. "Yes, I think that's right."

"In that case, I'd like to try an experiment. Is that all right?"

"What kind of experiment?"

I smiled as I patted her hand. "Meg, I'd like to kiss you."

Her eyes widened, and I knew she would agree. "Well, okay. I hardly know you."

"All the more reason."

I leaned across the table and gave her a five-second closed-mouth kiss on the lips. I leaned back and watched her with a smile on my face. Her eyes had closed, and when they opened, they flashed with excitement. She looked around. No one had noticed our brief kiss.

I waited. She broke the silence. "That was quite the experiment. What were your findings?"

"I'm going to wait before revealing my discovery, do you mind?"

She shook her head. "No, that's okay. I'm feeling a little flushed, can we go outside for a minute to get some air?"

"Certainly."

We stood and went out the door into the Louisiana summer heat. Fresh air was not to be had. She walked purposefully to the corner of the building, away from the entrance, and turned around to face me. I stood still. She came to me, stood on her tiptoes, put her arms around my neck, and kissed me deeply and hungrily for about 30 seconds. She released me, looked into my eyes again, then pulled me to her and repeated the kiss, with her tongue seeking mine as if it were starving. She was a great kisser, and her small mouth felt interesting.

Meg backed off and looked up at me, with a smile on her face. "Well, Dirk? What are your findings?"

I smiled back at her and paraphrased my long-ago friend Gabriella. "We will make love soon, Meg."

She kept smiling. "I agree with that hypothesis. We'd better get back inside."

We walked back to the door, holding hands. As we found our table, Ronni came over to check in.

"Hey, how are you two doing? That's so cute. Were you outside? Is it still hot?"

I chuckled. Ronni was in manic mode, half-crocked. "Yes, we went outside for a minute, it's still hot. We're fine. How is your table?"

Ronni grinned. "They keep buying me these buttery nipple drinks! They are soooo good!"

"Okay, why don't you have one more, and then we'll go to dinner. Meg is getting hungry."

She nodded. "Of course, Colonel Meg, Ma'am. I'll be back in a few."

I turned to Meg as Ronni bounced off a few chairs on the way back to her buddies. "Sorry to use you for an excuse. She'll get sick after too many of those."

Meg nodded. "That's fine, I could use something to eat soon. What shall we talk about in the meantime?"

I smiled. "How about the fact that I am very attracted to you?"

It was her turn. "I feel the same way, I can't explain it. Is this love at first sight?"

"More like lust at first sight. Meg, I'll be straight with you from the start. I'm not a long-term relationship kind of guy. Been there, done that."

Nodding, she said, "Me too. I'm too wrapped up in my career to give anybody enough time to be fair to them. Maybe later, but not now. I'm the hard-charging career woman officer at this point."

That made me smile. "A woman after my own heart. How about a weekend affair to start with, and see where that leads us?"

That got another smile out of her. "You're pretty sure of yourself, Mr. Caldwell."

"Let's check in with each other. You are no longer blushing, your tiny little hand that I am holding is now dry and warm, and your speech is confident and strong. You now know what you want and are trying to figure out how to achieve that. How am I doing?"

She grinned. "Pretty damned accurate. Your confidence is confirmed. I'm having trouble restraining myself from sweeping the drinks off the table, and having you right here, right now."

"I applaud your restraint. Even the casual bar has standards."

We both laughed, comfortable with knowing that we would be making love at the first opportunity. The sexual tension was palpable. We held hands under the table.

Ronni came back, swaying slightly. "Ready for dinner? I'm all caught up with buttery nipples!"

We stood and walked to the parking lot. A logistical challenge had emerged. Ronni and I were in her two-seat red sports car. I asked Meg, "Do you have a car?"

She nodded. "Yes, I'll follow you."

I drove sedately to the main gate and a few blocks on the other side was my favorite restaurant, Trejo's Mexican. Meg pulled in right behind us, and we entered, with me holding Ronni by the arm. She was very unsteady. Inside, I saw the manager and waved. He came up, grinning.

"Senor Dirk! Senorita Ronni! Welcome, welcome. Will you be three for dinner? Right this way. I believe your favorite table is available."

He led the way and seated us with a flourish. Ronni excused herself to the restroom, and I took the opportunity to talk to the manager quietly.

"Senor Enrico, thank you for your hospitality. This is Senorita Meg."

Enrico grinned and bowed. "Welcome, Senorita! I hope you enjoy your first visit."

I leaned close to Enrico. "Senorita Ronni is a little dizzy. If she asks for a margarita, please bring her one with no tequila."

He understood immediately. "Si, Senor. I understand fully. I will tell the waitress to bring a virgin margarita." He looked at Meg. "Excuse me, Senorita. I do not mean to be vulgar. This is the correct term for a margarita without alcohol."

She smiled and said in Spanish, "No hay problema, Enrico. Gracias por tu ayuda." (No problems, Enrico. Thanks for your help.)

Enrico smiled delightedly. "Ah, Senor Dirk! A beautiful woman who speaks Spanish! You are truly blessed!" He left and a few moments later, Ronni returned. The waitress appeared, and Ronni ordered the large margarita. I looked at Meg.

"Would you like to share a small one?" She nodded. "Would you order for us, please?"

She smiled and ordered our drink in Spanish. Ronni was impressed.

"Wow, Colonel! You speak Spanish. How cool is that!"

Meg smiled. "I took Spanish at the academy. Please call me Meg while we are socializing off base, Ronni."

Ronni nodded vigorously. "Yes, Ma'am. I mean Meg. Were you two holding hands a minute ago?"

I stepped in. "Yes, Meg was a little cold in the air conditioning."

Ronni nodded. "Damned straight." She was wobbly.

We chatted while waiting for our order. A server brought out a delicious-looking bubbly dish of Queso. "This is Queso Fundido, compliments of Senor Enrico."

"Ah, tell him muchas gracias!"

We enjoyed the queso and Ronni got restless. "Going to have a smoke until the food comes!" she announced and walked to the door.

Meg took the opportunity to put her hand on my bare leg below my shorts. She looked into my eyes and without thinking, I leaned in and kissed her. She smiled and returned the favor while Ronni was away. My groin was stirring in anticipation.

The food came. Ronni was nowhere in sight, so we started. After a few minutes, Ronni appeared holding a large, almost empty margarita glass. I involuntarily said, "Oh, shit!"

Ronni plopped down. "I stopped at the bar and got a drink. The one I had tasted like there wasn't shit for tequila. Got me a double at the bar!" She took a long pull and drained the big glass and started swaying. I left Meg and sat down beside Ronni, putting my arm around her. She started to close her eyes and almost passed out. I looked at Meg, who sat there expressionless.

I went into action. Waving at the waitress, I ordered the remaining food boxed up to go. Then I reached into my pocket for a credit card. Meg waved me off and put hers down. I started to get Ronni up and walk her out with some semblance of dignity. Meg followed us out. I just looked at her.

"I have to get her home, Meg."

"No problem, I'll follow you."

Propping Ronni up, we were back home in about 10 minutes, and after trying to get her to walk into the house, I gave up and threw her over my shoulder in a fireman's carry to the master bedroom. Meg followed us in.

Meg asked, "You seem to have done this before, what's the routine?"

"I undress her to her underwear and put a tee shirt on her, then put a trash can by the bed in case she gets sick."

Meg nodded grimly. "I'll undress her, get me a shirt."

Soon Ronni was on her side in case she vomited, and we retired to the living room.

I looked at Meg. "Well, that takes the romance out of the evening pretty quickly."

She laughed. "As a squadron commander, I see a lot of situations. Let's sit down and catch our breath."

We went to the living room and sat on the couch close to each other. I put my arm around her. "Where were we?"

She snuggled into me. "I believe you were thinking about kissing me."

"You are correct." I kissed her long and deeply. Our hands started to roam each other's bodies. I stopped and put some music on, smooth jazz instrumentals. I went to Meg and offered my hand.

She smiled at me. "Where are we going?"

"To the kitchen. Kick off your sandals. We're going to dance."

"In the kitchen?"

"Yes, it's the best."

We danced in the kitchen for a while, slowly and sensuously. I held her close, and she had her arms around my neck reaching up. The top of her head came to the center of my breastbone. I had to ask.

"Meg, honey? How tall are you? Just curious."

She had to laugh. "The Air Force Academy entrance minimum height is four foot ten inches. I was recorded as four foot ten inches and one quarter. I was stretching big time to get that."

"Well, I think you are a perfect size."

She laughed. "Thanks. I hear a lot of short jokes."

"Is Meg short for something?"

"Yes, Megan. My full name is Megan Juliana Devereaux."

"Wow, that's a mouthful!"

She laughed again and moved her arms to fit around my back. "My friends call me Meg, Megan, or MJ. You can call me any of those."

I smiled and bent down to kiss her. My hands roamed her back and ass. It was a nice, tight ass. I was looking forward to seeing it naked, bent over in front of me. "What do your lovers call you?"

She smiled up at me. "I don't have a lot of lovers, but any of those names work. I've heard 'Oh, God!' a few times."

I had to laugh. She had a great sense of humor.

"How do you like dancing in the kitchen?"

She pulled me in close. "I like it, it feels romantic. This is different from just ripping our clothes off and having hot jungle sex, which is what I want to do with you right now."

I laughed again. "How about a romantic dip in the hot tub, then hot jungle sex?"

She smiled. "That sounds fantastic."

I showed her my bedroom, then a chest of drawers in the third bedroom. "Here's a robe, and there are ladies' swimsuits in the top drawer. I'll go out and uncover the hot tub and turn it on."

"Great, I'll meet you out there."

I went out and got the hot tub going, and after a few minutes, Meg joined me. After looking around, she said, "Can we turn some of these lights off?"

"Sure." Soon we were on a dimly lit backyard covered patio.

She walked up the steps. I said, "I'll take your robe if you like."

"Thanks."

Facing away from me, she took the robe off, handed it to me, and went up the steps and down into the hot tub. Meg was naked under the robe. She got in, exclaimed at how nice the water felt, and smiled.

"Care to join me, Mr. Caldwell?"

"I would indeed, Colonel Meg."

I climbed into the hot tub and with considerable effort, kept my hands off her for the time being.

That didn't last long. She snuggled up into me, took my arm, and put it around her.

"You, sir, are overdressed."

"I can rectify that in a few seconds."

"Please do so. You are holding up the next phase."

I slipped my trunks off. "What's the next phase?"

She grinned. "Uninhibited foreplay leading to sexual activity."

"I support that."

I kissed her deeply, and she turned towards me. My hands roamed her naked body, enjoying the boobs, bare ass, and thighs inside and out, and tracing her labia with a finger. She moaned deep in her throat and her hands did the same to my body, giving my rigid cock some love as she caressed me all over.

I pulled her onto my lap facing away from me. Her legs straddled mine, spread just enough. My hands caressed her boobs, noting that the nipples were good-sized and fully erect. I ran my hand down her slender belly and went up and down her thighs. Then, I slipped a finger into her pussy, marveling at how tight it was. She was petite all over, She groaned and squirmed her hips as my finger found her G spot and massaged it. I then played with the clit and ran my finger up and down her labia, all the while playing with her boobs with the other hand, all the while kissing her neck and shoulders.

Her moaning and groaning were nonstop now as our foreplay went on for several minutes. Her hips moved into my hand as my fingers excited her pussy. She put her arms behind our heads, grasping my neck and gripping me tightly. She cried out.

"Dirk, I'm horny as shit! Put your dick in me!"

"Would you like to get out and go to the bedroom?"

"No, I can't wait!"

She rolled off me, then turned towards me, straddling me in the bubbling hot water. Meg reached between her legs and guided my cock to her labia, then used her fingers to spread the lips.

She gasped, "Be careful on the initial entry. Slowly, please!"

My cock was the entrance to the vaginal vault, and she lowered herself onto the swollen head of my dick. There was a lot of resistance.

She moaned, "Push a little."

I gave a little push with my hips and felt the labia part as my cock slid into the tightest pussy I had ever experienced in my life.

I was stunned. "Wow!"

She grinned at me. "I've heard that before. Are you just going to sit there?"

I answered by starting a thrusting rhythm into her. It felt fantastic. For a while, I thought I had entered her asshole, so I reached around to the anus to see that it was unoccupied, giving it a little circle to show that I appreciated it.

She moaned in appreciation. "You can put your finger in if you want."

I did, and soon was fingering her ass while fucking her and kissing her and stroking her boobs with my free hand while kissing her nipples. It did not take long for all this activity to come to a head.

After a few minutes, she cried out softly. "Mmmmm! Mmmmm! Oh! Oh! Oh! Mmmmm! Ahhhhhhh!"

Her body stiffened, her back arched, and I felt her shudder. Her orgasm was in full swing. I pulled my finger out of her ass and used that hand to caress her ass and back. She moaned again, then collapsed against me. After a moment, her head rose, and she sought my mouth for a passionate deep kiss. I was still stroking gently into her, and she realized I had not come yet.

"Oh, Dirk! You haven't come yet! What do you need to do?"

"How about if I lay you on your back on one of the seats?"

"Oh! Please do! Keep going! It feels great!"

I laid her down on her back, so I was facing her from above. She braced herself on the edge of the hot tub as I stroked away.

She gasped, "You can do it harder if you want!"

I was afraid of hurting her, she was so small. Pumping harder, after a minute, I felt my balls load up and I came in a torrent, sending cum deep into her tiny pussy.

"Oh, damn! That feels great!"

She stroked my hair. "I'm so glad you liked it."

I had to laugh. "Liked it is an understatement, dear girl."

"Should we get out of this hot water for a while?"

"Good idea, want to just sit on the edge of the tub?"

"Yeah, that would be good. I hope the neighbors can't see us."

I looked around. The neighbor's windows were dark, hopefully they were sleeping. I looked at my watch. She noticed.

"When I woke up this morning in New Orleans, I would have never guessed that I would be having an orgasm in a hot tub in Shreveport at 2100."

I had to laugh. "When I woke up here in this house this morning, I would have never guessed that I would be making love to a beautiful redhead in this hot tub this evening."

She smiled. "Aww, you're sweet. I'm no beauty queen, Dirk."

"C'mon MJ! You're cute as hell."

She reached up and touched my cheek. "So sweet. What's next?"

"Now we shower off the hot tub chlorine, reconvene in my little bed, and get ready for the next sex event."

"Sounds good. I'm pretty much in a nonstop sexual coma, thanks to you. Even though I just had a great orgasm, I want to try for another one."

I handed her the robe, and we made our way back inside. After looking in on Ronni, who was snoring away, we got in the shower together and had great fun washing each other off. I have a rule about showers, we both get to wash each other's private parts. She had a good time washing my dick, which responded. Her eyes got big.

"So soon? Man, you are some kind of virile!"

"You bring out the beast in me. What are you going to do about it?"

"Turn the water off so I don't ruin my hair, then stand by."

I turned the water off, and she knelt in front of me and took my cock into her small mouth. The blow job was very nice, with her rolling her tongue around my shaft and rimming my glans. I couldn't have asked for more. After a few minutes, she rose and smiled at me.

"How's that?"

"Wonderful! Can you please bend over in front of me and show me your tiny, yet shapely ass?"

She grinned. "Are we talking vaginal or anal?"

I pondered. "Vaginal now, anal sometime later. I'm falling in love with your tight pussy."

She laughed and turned her ass to me, shaking it provocatively. "Have at it!"

Once again, she spread her labia with her fingers, and I eased up to the entrance and gave a soft push to get in. I was almost overwhelmed by her tight, hot, pussy.

"Damn! MJ, that is fantastic!"

She giggled. "That's an advantage of being a small person."

I fucked her magnificent cunt for a few minutes, marveling at her shapely tight ass as I held her by her slender waist while reaching around and fondling her boobs. I then pulled out, and said, "Much as I want to keep going, I think we should go to the bedroom."

She grinned, turning around and kissing me.

"I thought you'd never ask!"

We toweled off quickly and went into my bedroom and climbed up on the twin bed.

As we lay down, she was smiling.

"What's that pretty smile for?"

"I'm happy in anticipation of getting some great head!"

"I'll do my best to live up to your anticipation."

I turned her to put her head on my pillow and knelt between her legs. She spread her legs in anticipation, and I admired the woman before me.

From her small head with dark red hair, her green eyes flashed at me beneath makeup that was still intact. A few laugh lines surrounded her mouth, and the beginnings of crow's feet were at the edge of her pretty eyes. Her facial features were round and normal for the skin type and structure. She had a cute spray of freckles across her nose and cheeks that I had not noticed before. Her skin was pale as most redheads are, and the pink lipstick accentuated her nicely shaped lips. A necklace complimented her smooth neck, and her shoulders were straight and athletic looking. Her breasts were larger than I expected, with a full B cup at least, with nice, big nipples. Her torso was slender, with a narrow waist enhancing the hourglass shape of her body, with a nice flare leading to the hips. The hips were beautiful, with enough ass to make a lovely round shape, melding into nicely shaped, smooth, and firm thighs. The vaginal area was crowned by a muff of ginger pubic hair, complimenting the slender lips of the labia. Her thighs merged into shapely calves, with a sprinkling of freckles from her muff to her ankles. The ankles were thin and shapely, leading to tiny feet with exquisite toes, with the second toe longer than the big toe on each foot. The toenails, like the fingernails, were painted a nice shade of red. She was beautiful. A body to admire for the ages. I was entranced.

She spoke. "Dirk? Are you okay?"

"I'm admiring your body. You're beautiful, Megan Juliana."

She blushed. "Thank you, Dirk. I'm all yours right now. Enjoy. After you give me some killer head, that is."

"Right!"

I knelt between her spread legs and gave the vaginal area a close inspection. The soft ginger hairs were thicker on top, with a thin layer on each side of the labia. I spread the lips with my fingers and put my tongue into the pink flesh. She gasped as I tickled the inside and ran my tongue north and south, tickling the small clit on the north side, and making a quick dart into the hole at the south end.

Ah, pussy. The sights and smells are fantastic. Hers had a little chlorine aroma left over from the hot tub, mixed with soap and my favorite, the anchovy sharp scent of fresh cunt. The lips glistened with my saliva and her natural juices, with more on the way as she became more excited. The hole was as tight as I had ever seen, with my tongue filling the entire hole as I pushed deeply in and curved it upwards, looking for the elusive G spot. All women have them, some are harder to find. Hers was found a lot closer to the vaginal entrance than I had expected. I heard a sharp intake of breath and a moan, accompanied by her hips squirming, and knew I had found it.

She exclaimed, "Oh, that's awesome! Do that spot again!"

I did, and her hips moved and she groaned. "Damn, that's good! I'm getting hot!" she gasped.

I was, too, and still had a raging erection that needed to be taken care of. I rose and reached for a small tin of Vaseline that I kept on the bedside table for these sorts of situations. I applied a small layer to the head of my cock and rubbed a little on the bottom of her pussy lips and into the hole. Kneeling so I was ready to enter, she once again spread her lips to make it an easier entry. I eased up to the hole and pushed gently, feeling the labia spread and her hole slowly yield as I went in. After the tight ring around the entrance, I was in and eased my entire length into her a little at a time and started pumping her gently.

Meg said, "Oh, that's nice. That's the way to do it. What was that stuff you put on me?"

"Plain old Vaseline. Works like a champ."

She smiled. "Simple solutions for simple problems! I like it. Keep that stuff handy, I may need it again this weekend."

"I like the sound of that. When are you leaving?"

She thought a moment, caressing my back and ass as I fucked her. "I was going to leave Sunday, but I can stay until Monday morning if I can find something to do."

It was my turn to smile. "I can find something to keep you occupied."

She closed her eyes and smiled again. "I certainly hope so. I'm feeling kind of tingly down there. Can you ..."

I answered her by picking up the pace and thrusting harder. "Is it okay like this?"

She had trouble answering while I was pounding away on her, but managed to say, "Deep and hard is okay, it's the entrance to the vagina that is so tight. Once it's in you can go to town!"

I was getting pretty horny by then, so I raised her legs up to get deeper and started drilling her harder. Her moans and groans let me know all was going well, and she pushed her hips into me, meeting every thrust. It felt fantastic, and I felt my balls preparing another salvo. I groaned heavily and let loose a load of cum deep into her pussy. She arched her back and pushed into me while letting out a low moan of ecstasy.

"Mmmm! Mmmm! Mmmm. Ahhhhh! Oh, that's nice. Mmmmm! Ahhhh! Oh, Dirk, I've come again! Wow!"

I stopped thrusting and lay on my elbows, trying to keep my weight off her, with my shrinking cock still inside her.

"Wow, Meg! That felt great!"

She grinned up at me. It was unusual to look down so far to see the face of my sex partner. "I've never had two orgasms so close together! What the hell is it with you, are you a sex magician?"

I shook my head. "It's all sexual chemistry. I can't explain it. I'm very turned on just being around you, and that makes it easier to have orgasms."

She nodded. "As soon as I met you, I felt it. Did you see my face flushing? I bet I was getting wet at the same time. Incredible!"

I kissed her and then eased out of her. As my dick came out, there was a noticeable plop as it came out of the tight entrance. I reached for a washcloth that was in the bedside table, and she used it to catch any drips.

She asked, "Should I put on the robe to go to the bathroom?"

I shook my head. "Ronni's out like a light. In the morning, though ..."

As she got up, she was smiling. "Are you assuming I'm spending the night in this twin bed with you?"

"Hey, it's hard to have wake-up sex if we don't wake up together."

"Good point."

She came back from the bathroom and climbed in next to me. The small bed made snuggling mandatory. As I put my arm around her, she threw a leg across mine and ran her hand over my chest. It was time for bedroom talk.

"So, tell me about this man I have flung myself at, letting you ravish my lily-white body."

"Shouldn't we have had this talk before you had sex with me?"

She laughed. "You were there, there was not a lot of time to talk before we started screwing."

"Well, I guess we could have waited …"

"Quit stalling. Tell me about yourself, please."

I gave her the short version. Grew up in California, joined the Air Force, and never went back. Started as an aircraft mechanic with Strategic Air Command, cross-trained to air refueling operator. Promoted early twice, held a lot of different management jobs, ended up in Louisiana, and then got out because I did not want to go to Scott AFB, IL, and a headquarters job I was being forced into.

She wanted more details. "Wives, children? Plans to get married again?"

I laughed. "One wife, early on. Never again. No kids. Don't plan on getting married, I don't even want to get serious. I plan on taking flight training and becoming a commercial airline pilot, that's kind of on standby until I can get an FAA Class One physical within a few weeks. It's in the works, but I'm kind of in no man's land right now. Tell me about Megan Juliana."

She laid her hand on my stomach and talked with her head leaning on my shoulder.

"I was born in Baton Rouge, the youngest of five kids. I'm the only girl. All my brothers are married and have kids, so I have a lot of nieces and nephews that I adore. Dad was military, an infantry officer in the Army during Vietnam. He went into finance stuff later. Mom is a manager at a bank. I got selected for the Academy and went into intelligence, then finance administration. I got picked to get my master's degree with the Air Force Institute of Technology. I've had some good assignments, in Germany and Korea, then heard the Louisiana Guard was recruiting females and offering fast track for promotion and command. I went to them as a Captain and am now a LtCol headquarters squadron commander. Never been married, although I came close a few times, so no kids. I really don't have time for a full-time serious relationship or to get married. I've seen other female officers go down that path and end up not fulfilling their goals."

I was stroking her leg and ass as she talked. "What's your end-state goal?"

She rose on an elbow and looked at me. "It sounds kind of far-fetched and ambitious, but my goal is to be a General Officer. I'd probably have to go to the Pentagon and serve some joint staff tours to get there. How does that sound to you, having known me for not even eight hours and having shagged me twice?"

"I think anyone who underestimated your drive and ambition better stand back or get run over."

She smiled. "How did you come to that conclusion only barely knowing me?"

"I've been around the Air Force for 20 years, and worked for and with some rising stars, and some that thought they were superstars but weren't. I'd bet you are a rising star. I like the way you talk and handle yourself when I am not distracting you."

"Thanks, Dirk. I also need to keep my reputation intact. I feel bad, but I can't take you back to my room at the visiting officer's quarters. I also should not be seen slinking back into my room at 0700 wearing the same clothes I had on for happy hour the night before."

"I totally get it, Meg. Will I be able to see you tomorrow?"

She sighed. "We have a dinner event with the Wing Commander and his staff tomorrow after work, I'll be wrapped up in that until evening. Maybe after that for a quick visit? Sunday afternoon, I'll have more time and can just come over here if that's okay with you. I have to ask, is Ronni ... discreet?"

"Like would she be able to keep her mouth shut about an Air National Guard squadron commander sleeping with a retired enlisted guy at her house? I wouldn't bet my career on it."

She frowned. "Crap!"

I stroked her leg some more. "I have confidence something will come up and it will all work out."

She kissed me. "I love an optimist! Okay, I have to run. I'll call you if I get free or get any ideas."

She got dressed, and I walked her out to her car. After a passionate kiss, she drove off, waving. I went back in and checked on Ronni. She was still asleep and snoring blissfully. I went outside, covered up the hot tub and straightened up the kitchen, then went back to bed. I smiled as I went to sleep. This Friday night had turned out pretty darned good.

Saturday

I awoke early for a Saturday and went to the kitchen to start a pot of coffee. After a while, Ronni came out dressed in her Air Force uniform looking okay considering how she went to bed. She poured a large mug of coffee and leaned against me with her head on my shoulder.

"Hey, Dirk. I feel like shit. Thanks for putting me to bed last night. I sort of remember it. Did you have sex with me while I was passed out?"

This was sort of a running joke with us. "Yeah, I violated every hole in your body and then put all your underwear back on you and a clean tee shirt and tucked you in."

"So that's why I feel a little rough this morning. Hey! How did it go with LtCol Devereaux?"

"She's nice. We had dinner while you took a nap, then I brought you back here."

"Yeah, sorry about dozing off during dinner. I told you she was super cute, am I right?"

"You were right. She's a peach."

Ronni sighed. "I'm already tired and I have to be at work all day and then talk about quality management at some dinner for the big wigs tonight. Yuck."

It sounded to me like it was the same thing Meg was attending. "Man, that's a long day."

"Well, it's my own damned fault I'm tired. What are you up to today?"

"Typical Saturday stuff. Catch up on laundry, wash the car, maybe do the back lawn."

"That would be awesome, but I'll help you with the lawn after work Sunday. Well, see you later." She gathered up her stuff and left.

I got my coffee and sat down to read the local paper after getting a load of clothes in the washer. An hour later I heard the garage door opening.

Ronni came breezing in. "Shit! I'm off to the airport. A guy was teaching quality management at the reserve squadron up in Indiana and came down with stomach flu, or food poisoning, or some shit and can't teach the class. That Wing Commander called my Commander and now I am headed up there to fill in for him first thing tomorrow and get their training knocked out since they have like 200 people waiting for it. I'm on a plane in two hours. I'll throw some clothes in a bag, grab my toiletries and run back by the office to pick up some training materials they are printing off for me. Can you please take me to the airport, so I don't have to leave my car there? And help me carry shit out of my office to the car?"

"Sure, Ronni. Let me shave and put on some better clothes if I'm going to your office."

She had to laugh. "You always dress for success when in a work environment. Forever the professional Senior NCO."

We got ready at the same time and rolled up to her office building in the Wing Headquarters building. I walked in with her and taped up the boxes of course materials, about the time the Wing Commander came by, with Meg in tow. She was wearing the camouflage fatigues of that era, called BDU or Battle Dress Uniform. She looked awesomely cute and professional. My heart skipped a beat as our eyes met.

He saw me. "Dirk! How the hell are you?" I knew the Colonel well and had taught a lot of his quality management training. We shook hands.

"Do you know Meg Devereaux?"

Our eyes met again, and we both smiled. It was not that many hours ago we were engaged in hot sex on my bed. "Yes, we had dinner together last night."

"Great! Are you taking Ronni to the airport? Did she tell you what is going on?"

I nodded. "Yes, on both counts, Colonel."

He looked at Meg. "I tried to hire Dirk here into our civil service quality officer position, but there is a damned freeze on civil service hiring." He looked at me. "Hey! I just had a flash! Dirk, are you free tonight? Ronni was going to speak about quality management at our leadership dinner tonight, but she will be in Indiana. Could you fill in and give us a 15-minute talk on quality management in the Total Force environment? Please? I'll buy your dinner."

I tried not to look too eager. "Sure, Colonel. I'll be glad to fill in. I'm retired. You had me at free dinner."

We all chuckled, and Meg had a sparkle in her eyes and a smile on her face.

The Colonel said, "Great, come to the Officer's Club at 1800. I'll have you seated at my table along with Meg."

"See you then. Oh, what's the dress code?"

He thought. "Uniform of the day for us, but you are technically a civilian. How about business casual?"

"Sounds good. I'd better get Ronni to the airport. See you later, Colonel." I looked at Meg. "See you later, Lieutenant Colonel Devereaux." She dimpled and blushed a little.

I grabbed the box of printed material and headed off to the airport. Dropping Ronni off, I pondered my good fortune. Free dinner with Meg, and the house is empty. Thank you, Cupid!

Saturday Night

Preparing for dinner, I shaved again, showered, and put on grey slacks and a light blue long-sleeved dress shirt. I decided against a tie because I hate them and got out my nice blue blazer from Hong Kong and ran the lint brush over it. Ready.

I arrived at the club 10 minutes early in accordance with my 20 years of military training. I was entering as the Commander and Meg arrived in his staff car. I waited and walked in with them. It's always good to be seen arriving with the Commander. Meg and the Commander still had their duty uniforms on, and I noticed how tiny Meg's combat boots were. She caught me looking at her and smiled with a blush as she looked away. Damn, she was cute!

We approached the head table, and the Wing Commander's executive officer came up to me. "Mr. Caldwell, it's good to see you again. I've seated you with LtCol Deveraux of the Louisiana Air National Guard on the Commander's right. Captain Ronni had some PowerPoint slides for her presentation, do you want to review them prior to dinner?"

That was a damned good idea. "Yes, indeed. Lead on, Captain."

After I checked over the slides, I took my spot at the head table next to Meg. I looked over at her and decided to tease her. I leaned over and said in a low voice, "Dinner two nights in a row with me. People will start to talk, Meg."

She leaned over to me and said also in a low voice, "If they knew how bad I wanted to fuck you right now, they would have plenty to talk about."

I smiled and nodded as if she had said something humorous. She was a pistol. I was starting to get an erection with the sexy talk. I hoped it would subside before I had to stand up and talk.

I made it through the dinner. A couple of times Meg had leaned over to pass the rolls or something and put her hand on my leg, one time sliding it up to my crotch. That was very stimulating.

I gave my presentation and got a round of polite applause. After the dinner, the Commander ushered us into the bar, where we all had an after-dinner drink and chatted for a while. At an appropriate time, Meg leaned over to the Commander.

"Sir? Mr. Caldwell has offered to drop me at my quarters on his way home. Would that be all right with you?"

He looked at his watch. "Of course, Meg. Dirk, thanks for taking Meg to her quarters, and thanks again for stepping in tonight. I swear that the moment the civil service hiring freeze is lifted, yours will be the first application I sign!"

I nodded. "Thanks, and it's my pleasure, Colonel. Good night."

Meg and I exited the dinner crowd and went to my car. I opened her door for her and resisted the urge to kiss her. Driving her towards the VOQ, I asked politely, "Where to, Ma'am?"

She had been squirming in her seat. "Give me your hand, please."

I did, and she placed it on her pussy, where she had unzipped her uniform pants and pushed her panties down. I felt damp pubic hair and some other nice things.

"Wow. That's nice. Are we going to your VOQ room?"

"Drop me at the VOQ. I'll get my car and meet you at Ronni's house."

"Don't forget to zip up before you get out."

She gave me a withering look. "Thanks for the reminder."

A few minutes after I got to Ronni's house, Meg pulled in. I greeted her with a deep kiss and held her tightly. She responded in kind.

"God! I've been wanting you to hold me all day!"

"Well, we're here in private now. Would you like to talk, or may I undress you while we ponder our next move?"

She grinned. "Dirk, my love? I don't have a lot to talk about right now. Please undress me, and we'll catch up later."

"You got it, MJ."

I had her out of her BDUs in no time, again marveling at the tiny boots. Soon, I had her naked on the living room couch and I was not far behind. My hands roamed her fantastic body, and I kissed her from her forehead to her toes. She was moaning in anticipation, and I applied my fingers and tongue to her everywhere I could reach. I knelt between her legs and spread them so I could get at her pussy. My tongue flicked into the pink flesh between her labia and she moaned in delight. She was getting hotter by the minute.

"Oh, Dirk! I'm ready! Put your cock into me!"

"Hang on a minute." I headed to the music station, and then put on my music playlist, starting with Joan Jett. She did great sex music, 'I Love Rock and Roll.' It was music to screw by. Then Anita Baker and 'Rapture' followed by 'Spooky' by Atlanta Rhythm Section, then back to Anita Baker with 'Sweet Love' followed by Martina McBride and 'Life #9.' If you haven't come by then, you're unconscious.

She exclaimed, "Yeah, that's great! C'mon, put it in me!"

"One more thing, I won't be a minute!"

I came back with a towel, a washcloth, and the Vaseline.

She saw what I was carrying and sat up so I could spread the towel under us to protect the couch. I dipped a finger in the Vaseline and put a layer on the head of my cock and gave the entrance to the vaginal vault a coating. She had other ideas.

Smiling, she said, "Put a little of that on my butt hole while you have it out."

I looked at her. "Why, MJ! What do you have in mind?"

"An unformed thought is roaming in my head, it may become clearer if you would please put your cock in me."

"Roll on your side for a sec so I can reach your ass."

She rolled over on her side and I was able to give her asshole a coating.

She said, "Since I'm on my side and lubricated, just do me like that!"

I moved my cock into position and straddled her down leg and raised the other. She guided me to the hole, and I pushed gently, feeling the ring of tissue around the entrance give way slowly and my cock slid in. She exclaimed as I did so.

"Oh! That feels so good! I've been wanting you in me all day! That Vaseline is such a good idea, it makes the entry easier."

I started humping into her, relishing the tight pussy and the great sideways position. She groaned and moaned as I put the meat to her. I held her leg up with one hand and played with her boobs with the other. She reached down behind my back and held my balls while I pumped her. We had hands and arms going everywhere, and they were all busy. It was quite stimulating.

After a few pleasant minutes, she wanted to change positions.

She gasped, "Sit down and let me straddle you!"

I pulled out and sat on the towel. She quickly got on my lap facing me and guided my rock-hard cock to the slippery entrance to her vagina. We made the entry carefully, which was easier this time as it was a little stretched out from use. As I went up inside Meg, she moaned loudly and started an intense hip rocking motion as she braced herself on my shoulders. While she enjoyed it, I suggested a change.

"Push your clit into me like you are trying to erase my pubic hair with it."

She looked at me like I was nuts until she changed the motion a little to what I had suggested. Her eyes got big.

"Oh, Dirk! That's awesome! Where in the hell did you ... Never mind."

I had to laugh. Gabriella's lessons were still in use. "I had an Italian sex tutor when I was younger."

She gasped out as she rode me hard, "That's just crazy enough to be believable."

I was thrusting up into her hard, and after a minute or two, she was close to orgasm. She had another request.

"Put your finger in my ass!"

Ah, that's what the Vaseline was for. I pushed a finger gently into her ass, and her moaning became louder and more strident as I slowly finger fucked her butt.

"That's it! Mmmmm! Mmmmm! Ahhhh! Ohhh! Yes! Mmmmm! I'm coming, Dirk!"

"I'm right behind you!" I felt my balls load up and seconds later was shooting hot cum up into Meg's miniature vagina as I felt her shudder. She slowed down the hip thrusting and came to a stop. I stopped as well. She collapsed onto me with her arms around my neck as we were both out of breath, breathing hard.

Meg pulled back, found my mouth, and started a long, passionate kiss. Then she took my head between her hands and kissed me all over my face.

"Oh, you wonderful man! I feel fantastic!"

"Me, too!"

She leaned into my chest and I stroked her back and ass for a while. Then she rose and said, "It's getting late, and I need to get back to the VOQ. Shall we plan tomorrow?"

"Yes, indeed."

She was running her fingers through my hair as she talked. "I have to be at work all day but can come straight over after. I'll go by the VOQ and change first. Do you want to eat in? I'll stop by the market I saw a block or so from here and get some stuff to cook."

"Eating here sounds good, but I don't want to put you on kitchen duty."

"Nonsense, I love to cook and don't have a man to cook for. Until now. That way we can stay here and be on our own schedule. Let me snoop in the kitchen first to see what kind of spices and stuff you and Ronni have. Oh! When is Ronni due back?"

"Monday afternoon."

"Great! I'll plan on spending the night with you and leaving here Monday morning. How does all that sound?"

I kissed her. "We have a plan."

"Good. I suppose I should get off you before you start another round ..."

"Almost too late. I'd better let you get up." My cock was stirring and liked being inside her.

She got up carefully, using the cloth to keep the drips in as she headed to the bathroom. I got up and found my underwear and put them on. She came out naked and started the process of getting her underwear and uniform back on. I loved watching her dress, and she smiled as I watched her.

Once dressed, she opened the kitchen cupboards and talked to herself as she ticked off in her head what she was looking for. "Okay, got it!"

She turned around and we embraced. It was interesting hugging an officer in a camouflage uniform. "Walk me out?"

I did and we kissed for a nice minute, then she got in and drove off like the night prior. The house was strangely quiet when I went back in.

Sunday

Meg called me during the day to check in and tell me her ETA. She whispered that she wanted to get out of there and come join me. I told her I was anticipating her arrival with great pleasure. She arrived at about 5:30 with a couple of grocery bags and an overnight bag, wearing civilian clothes, a nice blouse, and light-colored shorts. I helped her carry the items in and we hugged tightly and kissed for a while. My dick woke up as soon as she pushed herself up against me and I'm sure she felt it. She pulled back and looked up at me with a big smile on her face.

"I can tell you missed me!"

"More than you can ever imagine, my dear. What's in the bags?"

She was still smiling. "I'm going to make you my shrimp creole, dirty rice, a salad, and you can do garlic bread."

I was impressed. "Wow, you can do all that?"

"Yeah, it's my Cajun or as they say coonass upbringing, all us kids had to learn to cook. I also have ice cream for dessert."

"Have I told you yet today how much I adore you?"

She dimpled and stood on her tiptoes to kiss me. "No, but you may repeat that at any time. When do you want dinner?"

I looked at my watch. "Hmm. I have no set timetable. You?"

She was smiling radiantly. "I think we have time for a drink and a quickie, then you can help me with dinner."

"I hope you didn't say quick drink."

She chuckled deep in her throat. "You know what I said, Mr. Caldwell. Help me get the shrimp and a few things in the fridge, then we'll have that drink and the other thing."

"Do you like scotch? Many women don't, but I am guessing ...."

"Sure, that would be fine."

I had splurged too much of my meager income and had a nice scotch on hand. I put some soda in it, and we sat on the couch and toasted.

"To the end of the weekend and thanks in advance for cooking."

We sipped the scotch. She nodded her head. "Not too peaty, but with a good finish. Nice."

"I'm just so tickled you know about scotch. I need to know all about you. What else do you know?"

She laughed. "Hell, Dirk. My Dad was an infantry officer and I have four brothers. I know about a lot of guy stuff. Sometimes I'm around women jabbering away about some girly crap I don't care about and wonder what the hell their problem is."

I tried to be sly. "I have personal knowledge about one kind of girl stuff you know about."

She grinned. "You mean blow jobs?"

I about spit my drink out as she laughed at me. "Well, that is a good start ... What an icebreaker."

We set our drinks down and kissed for a while. This raised our temperatures as evidenced by clothing items that had to be removed. In a few minutes, we were in a state of undress and able to fondle a lot of each other's bare flesh.

She had her shorts on but unzipped, with nothing on her upper torso. I was giving her boobs and nipples some love while she rubbed my now erect cock. She panted out, "Pull my shorts down and bend me over the couch. Please say you have the Vaseline handy!"

"I do!" I had prepositioned the petroleum jelly and some washcloths on the end table. One cannot be over-prepared in a volatile situation such as this. I pulled her shorts down, and she rolled over to face the couch. I lubricated the head of my dick and her entrance area.

I pushed my cock up to her labia as she guided me to the tight entrance. Once again, I eased into the hole and felt it slowly allow me in. What a feeling! I went all the way in and started thrusting into her as she moaned and groaned. I admired her tiny, shapely ass as I pounded into her. I was enjoying the riding time and things were about to become critical when she spoke.

"Dirk, honey! I'm going to want some head later, don't come inside me unless ..."

"I get it. I'll just pull out and come on your back."

"No! Just put the head in my ass and come that way!"

Wow, that would be different. She was already handing me the Vaseline. I put a finger in and got enough, then circled her asshole, then worked it in a little with much moaning from her. Within a minute, I was ready to come.

I managed to gasp out, "I'm about to come!"

"Okay, just the head!"

I had the concept and now was faced with the execution. I pulled out of her pussy and lined up my dick with her asshole and pushed forward a little. This was similar to her tight pussy entrance. I got most of the head in and then my balls let go, so I shot a load of cum mostly into her ass but also some leaked out around the imperfect seal. Oh, well, at least the pussy was still clean.

I had groaned heavily as I came and was now catching my breath. She shook her ass a little, which was fun as my dick was still partially in her asshole. I had to confess.

"This is the first time I have tried that maneuver, and I've made a mess."

She giggled. "It was a spur of the moment idea. I wanted to see what your dick felt like in my ass, but not the whole thing."

"I'm not sure I got enough in there for you to make up your mind. Let me wipe you off before you move."

I wiped her down, then pushed the cloth between her butt cheeks. "You may want to hold that there for the walk to the bathroom."

She rolled off the couch and stood, the cloth protruding from her butt. "How not romantic!"

I pulled my shorts and shirt back on and heard her from the bathroom door. "Can you loan me a tee shirt?"

"Yep." I got a shirt and handed it to her, and she came out a moment later wearing it. It was like a tent on her tiny frame. "That may be a little big on you."

She laughed and did a pirouette to model it.

"I'd better get started on dinner, or we'll get distracted again and never eat."

"I'll make us another drink while you are doing that."

Watching her start preparing the meal from the kitchen bar stools, we visited and swapped stories about different military situations we had been in. We talked and talked until she looked up with a smile.

"This is really fun."

"I'm enjoying watching you work."

"Come over here and put your arms around me, I'm lonesome for you."

I complied, and with me hugging her from the back, she raised her head to be kissed, so I did. She chuckled.

"Someone's happy to see me."

She had felt my half-erect dick against her back.

"A couple of us are."

"Mmmm. Rub the head of your dick up and down my butt crack, I want to see what that feels like."

I unzipped and pulled my dick out, then raised the tee shirt to see her naked ass.

"Why, MJ! You have forgotten your panties!"

She giggled.

"You're kind of low, raise up on your tiptoes so I can get at it."

She raised up on her toes while leaning against the counter. I ran the head of my dick up and down the butt crack. She moaned a little.

"Careful not to dislodge that wad of toilet paper. Someone shot some cum up my butt, and it's still oozing."

"Guilty as charged."

She leaned back into me. "Don't forget about my boobs."

I reached under the tee shirt with both hands and caressed her nice boobs, tweaking the nipples a little as she sighed and moaned.

"I'd better stop that and let you finish."

She pulled the shirt back down and went back to sautéing or whatever the hell she was doing. I found a bottle of red wine and poured us each a glass.

We sat down to dinner, and I exclaimed about the food.

"MJ, you're a hell of a cook!"

She smiled. "I'm glad you like it."

We chatted some more, and at a pause in the conversation, she looked thoughtful.

"I think I want to try anal sex."

I almost dropped my fork. "That's not what I expected to hear during dinner."

Laughing, she said, "Sorry! It just came to me. So far in my life, there has been one finger and one dick in or near my ass, both yours. I want to try it with you."

"Can we finish dinner first? This is really good."

She laughed so hard I thought she would choke.

"Damn, you are so funny! Can I ask you about it?"

Shrugging, I said, "Sure. What would you like to know?"

"Well, do you do anal sex with your other girlfriends?" I must have looked defensive. "C'mon, I know you have girlfriends. Do they like it"?

I thought for a minute. "A few love it and can't get enough of it, others don't mind it but like it only once in a while because it's a bit kinky, and others want to try it but then say never again. A few don't want to even try it."

"Hmmm. Which category do you think I'll be?"

"I'm afraid to hazard a guess."

She nodded. "I'm not sure either, but I want to try it with you, I don't know why. Is it going to hurt?"

"I'm not going to lie. There is an intense feeling the first few times, some women call it pain, and others call it pressure. The worst is getting past the anal sphincter, once I'm past it will feel not as intense. Some like it, some don't. The second you say you don't like it, I'm out of there."

She nodded thoughtfully.

We finished dinner without any more intimate sexual discussions, and both cleaned the kitchen.

"That was fun, Dirk. I like cooking for you."

"I liked it a lot. You can come up to Shreveport and cook for me any time."

She grinned. "If I come to Shreveport, it will be for more than cooking."

"That sounds wonderful, exciting, and fulfilling."

I took her hand and walked her back to the kitchen. "Time for barefoot dancing in the kitchen."

She smiled broadly, "Aww. How romantic."

We danced slowly for several minutes, with our arms around each other, not saying a word, and then we kissed deeply. Then we sat back on the couch with another glass of wine.

After drinking a few sips, she put her glass down and took my glass from me. "That was very nice. What shall we do now?"

I tried to look innocent. "I don't know. Watch TV, play cards, talk ..."

"Kiss some more? Or watch the news and kiss during the commercials."

"I like the way you think."

We watched the news and kissed during the commercials. It was a great way to watch TV.

The phone rang, and Meg looked at me. "It's always for Ronni." Then the answering machine picked up and I heard Ronni's voice start to leave a message, so I picked up the handset next to the couch.

"Hi, Ronni. How's Indiana?"

"Hey, Dirk. It's fine. The boys and I hit the club after my class, and we are going somewhere to dinner. You used to be here, where should we go?"

"It's a ways to either Peru or Kokomo, you'd do better to eat at the club and not have to drive."

"Oh, okay. Hey, can you pick me up at the airport tomorrow at about 1730? I'm on Delta from Atlanta."

"I'll be there."

"Thanks, you're a doll. How are things there? How were your dinner and presentation?"

"No issues. I used your slides, and it went fine."

"Cool. Okay, we are heading to dinner. See you manana." She rang off.

Meg looked at me. "Did she ask about me?"

I shook my head. "She's distracted by the Indiana guys."

The news finished, and we were starting to get wound up with all the kissing.

I turned the TV off, looked at her, smiled, and said, "Okay, you sexy little redhead, get your ass on my lap. It's time to pick up the pace."

She maneuvered to be on my lap with her legs to the side and her arms around my neck. I reached under the tee shirt and found her naked ass and ran my hand up and down the inside of her thighs. She smiled and started tugging on my shirt. "Once again, Mr. Caldwell, you have way too many clothes on."

"I am so sorry." I pulled off my shirt and tossed it aside. I then pulled up her tee shirt until I had access to her boobs. I started fondling and kissing them. Her nipples were big in diameter, about twice the size of a pencil eraser. With my licking and nibbling, the nipples were soon standing at attention and were fun to tweak with my tongue.

Meg was working on getting my shorts unfastened and her hand down in my underwear. She found my cock and started by wrapping her tiny hand around it and stroking it. That felt great and made my dick swell quickly.

After a few minutes of that, I put a hand on her pussy and tickled the labia, getting a groan out of her. Then I had an idea.

"New thing to try. Dancing while naked!"

"Ooh! I like the way you think. Get rid of those shorts, mister!"

Now I was naked, and we walked to the kitchen, where I bent down and slowly and sensually pulled the tee shirt off with my teeth. She liked that a lot. As the shirt came off over her head, my boner was up against her torso with our height difference. She knelt down a little and pushed her boobs together around my throbbing cock and rubbed up and down. That felt really nice.

"Ooohh, Meg. That feels wonderful."

She smiled and stood up, our arms went around each other, and we danced again. The feel of our naked bodies against each other was very erotic as we swayed around the kitchen. My hands roamed her ass and back, while hers went up and down my thighs and ass. We spent several minutes doing this, and then at about the same time were ready for more. She stood on her tiptoes and pulled my face to hers for a deep and passionate kiss.

She kissed my neck, cheek, and ear, then whispered, "I'm ready to try it in my ass."

I pulled back and smiled at her. "Let's do it."

I walked her back to the couch and towel, turning her around and bending her over as she put her knees on the floor and laid her torso on the couch. I reached for the Vaseline and applied some to her anus, working it in as she groaned. After finger fucking her ass for a minute, I told her, "Here comes two fingers."

She nodded her head. I put the second finger in and worked them in and out as she gasped, then moaned. I could feel the anal sphincter relaxing a little.

"I'm going into your pussy first while I have two fingers in your ass."

She nodded again. I had some Vaseline on my dick already, so I eased up into her labia, and she helped things by spreading her lips. I pushed in and soon had my dick all the way up her sweet pussy while two fingers worked her ass. I could feel my dick with the fingers I had in her ass. It was cool.

After slowly fucking her pussy for a few minutes while she writhed and moaned, I pulled my dick out of her pussy, my fingers out of her ass, and pushed the head of my dick up against her asshole.

"Here we go. Any time you want me to stop, just say so, loud and clear."

"Okay. I'm ready. I think. Oh, jeez, why am I doing this?"

I rubbed her ass cheeks for a minute with my dick up against her anus while she gathered her courage. After a minute, she made up her mind.

"Okay. Fuck it. Go ahead. Put it in my ass!"

I answered by starting to push in while pulling her butt cheeks sideways to help things along. My cock pushed into her ass, and I could feel the sphincter stretching a little, then the head was in. I stopped.

"Oh, wow! You weren't kidding. That is intense. Wait a minute!"

I reached around and played with her boobs for something to do while I waited.

She moaned, then said, "Okay, push in a little more."

I pushed in a couple of inches and waited.

"Oh, my! That is some kind of feeling. Can you wait again?"

"Sure."

After a minute to let things ease up, she said, "Okay, keep going."

I pushed in some more. She didn't complain, so I pushed a little more.

I checked in with her. "How are you doing?"

She gasped, "This is an incredible feeling. It's a lot of pressure. How much more can you go in?"

"A couple or three more inches, maybe."

"Damn. Can you pull it out and back into where you are now?"

"Sure thing. I'll go in and out gently a few times."

I did, and she groaned.

"Okay, I think that's as far as I want it right now. Keep going in and out."

"You got it. " I gently ass fucked her for a few minutes.

She said, "You know, it's easing up a little. Push in some more. Fuck it, I'm almost there. Push it all the way in!"

I eased in until my pubic hair was up against her ass cheeks.

"That's the whole thing."

"Damn! That is a lot! Go ahead and pump me a little. Can you come like this?"

I started a slow, sexy thrusting rhythm. "Yeah, I'm only a couple of minutes from coming. How are you doing?"

She was gasping. "Okay, I guess. Go ahead and keep going until you come."

"Only if you're sure."

"Yeah, I'm okay. Do women come during anal sex?"

I immediately thought of Darla and how she loved to orgasm during anal sex. "Some do. Most don't."

"Okay. I'm not feeling like it, too many other feelings happening. Go ahead and come."

I was pretty close, and after I fondled her boobs a little more, felt a surge of cum racing towards the finish line.

I was groaning. "I'm coming!"

My cock spurt cum deep into her ass, and I held her small waist tightly as the spasms of hot juice went out of my dick. I tried not to push in any harder.

She exclaimed. "Wow! I could feel your dick get harder and then swell a little as you came. That's wild. Okay, you can pull out now."

She was ready to have me out of her ass. I eased back, and as my cock came out, an audible plop was heard. I had a cloth ready and wiped her butt hole, then pushed it between her cheeks to keep the dribbles contained. She got up off her knees and faced me.

"That was wild! I'm glad it was with you, I trusted you not to hurt me. I think you were as gentle as you could, but it still hurt, kind of in a good way. I think I'm in the every now and then category. Maybe on your birthday, or New Year's Eve."

I kissed her. "You were brave to try it."

"This is the weekend of trying new things and being reckless. Let me hit the bathroom."

"How about recuperating in the hot tub?"

"Oooh, yeah! I'll be out in a minute. Where's that robe?"

"I'll lay it on my bed for you."

I went into Ronni's bathroom and gave my dick a good wash. It was getting kind of red from all the activity. I smiled. That was not a bad thing.

Soon we were relaxing in the warm bubbly water. I put my arm around her and admired her cute naked body.

"How's your bottom?"

She grimaced. "I can feel that it's a little sore."

"Here, I'll hold you up. Turn so your butt is lined up facing a water jet and put your heels over the edge. It'll blow right on your sore butt."

I had her by the waist as she directed the water up her butt crack.

"Hey! That's pretty nice. I can feel it in my vagina as well, an added benefit. Reach down there and spread my lips a little while I hold onto your legs."

I complied, and she moaned. "That's very, very nice. Can I stay like this for a minute?"

"You bet. Do you want me to finger you?"

"Oh, what a good idea! Yes, please!"

I changed my grip on her waist with one arm and used my free hand to start working over her pussy. I ran my finger up and down the lips and then tickled her clit, With the warm bubbles surrounding it she was especially sensitive to stimulation. Meg started moaning as I tickled her, then when I slipped my finger into her hole and went straight to her G spot, her hands gripped my legs hard and her hips bucked and wiggled.

"Oh! Dirk, that's getting me wound up pretty fast! Oh, my! Oh!"

I thought she was still excited from anal sex, and this got her motor running quickly. She braced her feet against the edge of the hot tub and pushed into me. In turn, I pushed her in closer to the edge, to make the stream of water more powerful and to compress her legs into a more sensuous stance. It seemed to be working.

"Oh! Oh! Mmmmmm! Oh! Mmmm! Oh, my! Oh! Oh, Dirk, I'm coming! Ohhhhhh!"

I kept working her G spot until her body shuddered, then I went to gently massaging her clit and put pressure on her pussy. She had collapsed into my arms and was limp.

I turned her around as I sat on one of the seats and put her on my lap. She wiggled around until she was straddling me while facing me put her arms around my neck and smothered me with kisses as the warm water swirled around us.

"Damn! This is indeed a weekend of firsts! Sex in the hot tub, couch sex bent over, anal sex, naked dancing, and an orgasm in the hot tub! What the hell is left?"

"We'll think of something."

"Kiss me while you're thinking!"

"Yes, Ma'am."

I kissed her long and deeply. She ran her fingers through my hair and massaged my neck while I played with her ass and ran my hands over her back. After a few minutes of that, she pulled back and looked at me with a smile.

"Really, Caldwell?"

I tried to look innocent, but my boner gave me away. "You do things to me ..."

She raised and guided me to her labia. "No Vaseline, but water is slippery. Be careful."

"I will." I pushed gently into her and was soon all the way in her tight pussy.

She started rocking her hips on me as I thrust into her.

"Caldwell, you just had anal sex and came like 15 minutes ago, and you're hard already and I am letting you fuck me like we hadn't done it in a year. What the hell is it with you?"

"I feel somewhat attracted to you, can you tell?"

She grinned as she fucked me. "It's a hell of a compliment, I'll tell you that. I'm flattered that you are so turned on, and I am, too!"

"You are sexy, have a fantastic body, are cute as hell, and are fun to be with. Those are all a turn-on."

She laid her head against my neck as we rocked together. "You say the sweetest things."

I concentrated on what I was doing and looked at her after a few minutes. Her eyes were closed, and her lower lip was between her teeth.

"You okay, Meg?"

She smiled dreamily and looked at me with those pretty green eyes. "Dirk, I don't believe it, but I'm tingling down there again. Can you play with my boobs? I think I want to try again."

"With pleasure!" I started fondling and nibbling her boobs while stroking her ass as she bounced up and down as I pumped her vigorously.

She was gasping now. "Oh, oh, oh! I'm so close! Oh, my!"

I reminded her, "Push your clit into me like you are erasing my pubic hair."

"Oh, yeah. Oh! Oh! I'm so close. Ahhhhh! Oh, my!"

I circled her anus with a finger.

She perked up. "Stick your finger in a little!"

I was sucking her boobs, pumping into her, and fingering her asshole all at the same time while she was grinding her pussy into me.

She was shouting now. "Oh! Mmmm! Oh! Oh! Ahhh! Oh, God! Oh, God! I'm coming AGAIN! Ahhhhhh!"

I hoped the neighbors had their TVs on loud. We were making a racket. I was coming about the same time.

"Oh. Meg! I'm coming again. You are so sexy!"

She collapsed onto me as she shuddered. She looked up with a grin, panting from exertion.

"I'm sorry to have yelled. I was just a little bit excited. Damn! I have never done that in my life! An orgasm right after I had one? Amazing!"

I stroked her hair. "I'm proud of you, honey. And you got me hard, and I came again, you sexy wench! You're incredible!"

We held each other with the water swirling around us. Finally, I came to my senses.

"We'd better get out of this hot water."

"Oh, yeah. We're going to be prunes."

We got out and I put her robe on her. We staggered into the house and went straight into the shower to rinse the hot tub water off. It was very pleasant and even though we kissed and did a good job of washing each other, neither of us had an urge for more sex. We were fucked out.

She rummaged in her overnight bag and came up with a conservative set of pajamas, matching top, and shorts. She looked at me sheepishly. "All I brought was everyday pajamas. I didn't think I was going to need anything sexy."

"Dear girl, you don't need to have a sexy nightgown on to be desirable. You very obviously turn me on like a light switch."

She came to me and hugged me. "You are so sweet."

We went back to the living room and collapsed on the couch. I had on a tee shirt and gym shorts. I lay on my side and turned the TV on to some comedy show, and she lay in front of me with her back to me, wiggling into me. I put my arm around her.

"Are you warm enough, Meg?"

"Mmm, yes. You are a heat engine. I don't need a blanket."

We both dozed off within minutes and got a nice nap.

About the time the late news was on the weather forecast, I woke up as she was coming back from the bathroom. She plopped down next to my head and maneuvered so my head was on her lap. She stroked my hair as we watched the weather. When it went off, I said, "Looks like your weather will be good for your drive home tomorrow."

She nodded absently, then perked up. "Hey! We've got ice cream!"

We went into the kitchen, and I got out one bowl. She looked at me funny.

I laughed. "You must always share dessert with your lover."

She shook her head. "Is that more wisdom from the Italian chick?"

"Yep. That was one of her sayings. It works out well for intimacy and weight control." She gave me a look. "I'm talking about me, not you. You have a fantastic body. I'm trying to keep my belly under control."

I was forgiven. "That sounds fine. I will share dessert with my lover."

She dished out a healthy serving and pulled a bottle of chocolate sauce from the fridge. "You guys already had this."

"Ooohh! Nice."

We sat next to each other at the table so we could share, which was kind of fun.

Meg was curious. "Tell me about this Italian chick that was your sex tutor."

I thought for a minute. How do you explain Gabriella? "She and I met while I was an E-5 boom operator in Indiana about 15 years ago. We had an instant attraction to each other. We hooked up the next weekend and went down to Indianapolis together to work with the Ferrari racing team. She was an advertising VP from Chicago. I went along to meetings with her and even got picked up as a consultant to the race team for a while. It was heady stuff for a 25-year-old Staff Sergeant. She was older by about eight years and had seen a lot and done more than I would have ever imagined. She wasn't shy about helping me improve my very basic techniques in the bedroom, and would say things like, 'Dirk, tell your women to do this' and those tips were much appreciated. She was a pistol. We drifted apart after a great summer, and last I heard she was in South America."

Meg was staring at me. "Wow. What a story. You were one lucky Staff Sergeant."

"Oh, yeah, I was. She was a bombshell. Everywhere we went, heads turned."

"Did you love her?"

I thought for a moment. "I did, as a dear friend. We knew going in that there would be no long-term relationship, but my little heart thought it was love for a while. It was really lust and good friendship."

Meg sat quietly for a moment. "I suppose we are in the same fix. Friends with lust instead of love."

"I think a good way to think of it is I can love you but not be in love with you."

She smiled. "I like the sound of that. You can have the last bite."

"Now, that's a friend."

She unbuttoned her pajama top as I watched with interest. Smiling at me, she pulled the top apart to show her boobs. She coyly said, "Oh, Dirk! I've spilled some chocolate on me, can you help me get it off?" Then she dribbled a few drops of chocolate on one nipple. I gaped in amazement.

"You'd better hurry before it drips! No hands!"

I got the hint and bent over to lick the sauce off the nipple as she moaned. Then she dribbled some on the other one as well. "Oh, look! There's some on this one, too!"

I went to that nipple and did a good job of cleaning it off as well. This was fun!

"I think the first one still has some on it. You'd better check it."

To be thorough, I sucked the nipple and ran my tongue around the erect nipple several times as she moaned in delight. Then I went back and did a good job on the other side. I think it cleaned up very nicely. I rose.

"All clean."

"Good job! Oh, I see some has gotten on your shorts. You'd better take them off, and the underwear, too."

I took off the shorts, and she dribbled a little of the sauce on the end of my semi-awake prick. "I'll get this off for you." She commenced to lick the glans clean and took the now wide-awake dick into her mouth and wrapped her tongue around the shaft as she bobbed her head up and down. I loved it but did not know where we were going with this.

After a few very pleasant minutes, she pulled back and stood up, putting her arms around my neck while she stood on her tiptoes.

"Let's go to the bedroom and do the sixty-nine until we come or fall asleep."

"That's a plan I agree with!"

We walked back to my room, and I took a look at my pitiful twin bed. "Let's borrow Ronni's king-sized bed."

She looked at me. "Are you sure?"

"Yeah, I'll wash her sheets tomorrow and remake her bed before she gets home. She'll never know the difference."

She smiled coyly. "Have you done this before?"

I looked directly at her. "Never ask a question if you can't stand the answer."

Meg put her arm around me. "Sorry, Dirk. Just female nosiness."

We pulled the half dozen or so pillows off the bed and climbed in. I assumed my station at her crotch, and she prepared to take me back in her mouth. She had a question.

"I've never actually done this. Who's on top?"

"I think you will like it better on top. You can move your head around more easily and my balls won't hang in your face. But first, let's do this. I'll have you sit on my face."

She grinned. "I'm learning all kinds of new stuff this weekend! Put me where you want me."

"I'll just lay down, and you come and put your crotch in my face, straddling my neck facing towards my head. Then just sit up straight, wiggle, squirm, and do whatever you want while I give you head. Then after a while, you'll go face down to my crotch and do your thing while I keep giving you head."

She was still grinning. "Sounds like a win-win."

Meg assumed the position, and I very quickly had a face full of warm, aromatic pussy. I loved it. The scent of hot tub and soap lingered, and I hoped the sperm I had shot up there a while back had left. I enthusiastically started in on her pussy, licking north to the clit and wrapping my tongue around it like a straw and sucking gently. This got a good reaction from her, so I went south and licked my way into the vaginal vault and tickled the tight entrance to her hole, then went in and curled my tongue to get at the G spot. She moaned and squirmed as I hit the target.

After a few minutes of groaning and squirming, she dismounted and without a word spun around and took my cock in her mouth while scooting her pussy back to get more licking. This time, north was south and vice versa. I had to work a different angle to get my tongue to the G spot, but I made it work. I licked up and down the slit while she moaned and squirmed. I was hitting the right spots, and she was getting hotter than a firecracker.

"Oh! Oh! Yeah, that's it! I'm so close! Oh! Oh! Mmmmm!"

I reached an arm down and managed to find a boob to play with. She rose a little to facilitate that while still sucking my cock, and I got ahold of the nipple and squeezed it, and fondled the boob. That sent her nearly over the top, then with my other hand, I reached over my head to her asshole and circled that with my finger.

She went crazy with all that attention, and cried out, "Mmmmm! Oh! Oh! I'm coming, oh God, I'm coming again! Oh! Oh! Ahhhhhhh!"

She collapsed against my chest but was nice enough to use her hand to pump my cock while she was coming, and the thought of that tiny hand with the painted nails wrapped around my cock was making me hot.

She rested a minute, then sat up and scooted her hips down to my crotch area, raised up, and put my cock against her sopping wet pussy. She lowered herself until the head of my dick was against her tight hole, then gasped out, "Push a little!" I did, and my cock was in her. She was in the reverse cowgirl position, having mounted me while facing away. She rode me sitting up straight for a while, then bent over and braced herself with her hands on my ankles. She was bent over with my cock up her as she rocked her hips back and forth.

She exclaimed with raspy breath, "As hard as you want to, Dirk!"

I thrust up into her with all I had. The sight of her tight little perfectly formed ass jiggling in front of me, along with her pale skin and hourglass slender waist, with her red hair bobbing each time I pounded into her was getting to be too much. My balls could take no more, and I could feel the load rising from deep in my balls and heading for my cock. I shot a load of hot cum into her dripping cunt as I groaned loudly.

She collapsed again, laying on my legs with her ass facing me. It was an incredible sight. We both caught our breath for a while, then she sat up and extricated herself from my wet cock, then came around and lay against me, still breathing hard. I stroked her hair and back as she rested quietly while running her fingers through my hair.

She raised her head to me. Sweat had formed on her forehead and her upper lip. I kissed it away as she grinned at me. "Damn! I've never come so much in my life! I am absolutely worn out but feel fantastic! How about you?"

"I'm pretty well fucked out, Meg. We have had some great sex today. That chocolate thing was really nice, and you doing the reverse cowgirl was great!"

She smiled. "It seemed like the thing to do, and since you like it from behind ..."

"That was perfect. You are so frigging sexy."

"Aww. Thanks. I vote for cleaning up and going to bed and talking until we go to sleep."

"I like it. Ladies first."

We reconvened back in the bed, with her wearing the pajama outfit and me in a tee shirt and underwear. She curled up into me and threw a leg over me. Sighing into my neck, she said, "This has been a fantastic weekend. Can you come to New Orleans with me so I can cook for you, we can dance in the kitchen, and make love about 20 different ways?"

"That sounds like fun."

She sighed again. "When should we see each other again, Dirk?"

"I have a pretty open schedule, I work in the simulator most UTA weekends, this one is unusual in that I did not have to work. Your unit is probably on a similar schedule. I hope to be getting my FAA physical soon, then finding a flight school to train at, and hopefully stay on as an instructor and build flying time."

"Sounds like sooner than later would be best."

"I think so. Let's look at your Day-Timer calendar tomorrow and pick a weekend in the near future.

She rose and looked at me. "How did you know I have a calendar like that?"

I had to laugh. "I've been around a lot of you organized go-getter officers. You have to have one to keep your life straight."

Giggling, she lay back down on me. "You know me so well already. Are you a snuggler?"

"Yep, I love it."

"I'm so glad you are. I love snuggling in bed."

I looked at my watch, it was getting late. "What time do you have to leave in the morning?"

She pondered that. "I need to go by billeting and check out, that won't take a minute. If I'm on the road by 1100 that would get me home by 1600 or so. No need to set an alarm clock since Ronni won't be home until later."

"Sounds good. I'm fading fast." I kissed her. "See you in the morning."

"Good night, Dirk."

Monday

In the morning, I awoke to an empty bed. I did the usual routine and went to find Meg. She was sitting on the couch in her pajamas having coffee, watching the news on TV. She looked up at me and smiled. "Hey, sleepyhead."

"Hey yourself. Somebody worked me hard yesterday, I needed restorative sleep."

I got some coffee and sat down beside her and kissed her. She curled up against me and we watched the news for a while in silence. After it went off, she asked, "Done with your coffee?"

I looked in my cup. "Just about. Why?"

She smiled sweetly. "It's time for goodbye sex. We can use the bed again, then I'll help you get the sheets washed before I go."

"You are indeed a planner. I love it."

We stood, and I used the opportunity to reach under her pajamas and cop a feel of some naked flesh. I caressed her ass and back, then ran my hands around the front, unbuttoning her top, then cupping her boobs in my hands. She was busy running her hands under my shirt, returning the favor.

Smiling, she said, "Let's go to the bedroom."

"I love it when you say that."

We lay on the bed, and I finished undressing her. We caressed each other, and after a few minutes, she said, "You don't need to do a lot of foreplay, Dirk. I just want you in me one more time before I go."

She reached for my cock and smiled again. "Looks like he is ready."

I put my hand on her pussy and slid a finger in. "So are you. But I'll get the Vaseline to make the entry easier."

She sighed as my finger tickled her G spot. "Ever the considerate lover."

I greased her tight entry hole and my dick, then knelt between her spread legs and put the head of my cock against the hole and pushed forward easily. I pushed until I was buried in her. She gasped with pleasure. I lay there for a minute, relishing the feeling. She waited patiently, understanding the moment. I then kissed her and started an easy thrusting rhythm. She gently pushed her hips into me as I pushed into her. Stroking my legs and ass, she sighed and said, "This is nice."

"Yes, it is."

We make slow and sexy sweet love for several minutes, each enjoying the other's body and the feeling of intimacy. Her hips started to squirm a bit, and some moaning came from her mouth.

"Dirk? I want to get on top, I'm feeling some tingling down there and ..."

"Say no more, I'll roll over with me still in you."

She smiled. "Cool!"

I managed the maneuver, and she drew her legs up and straddled me, immediately starting to push her clit into me. I thrust harder into her, and her moaning became constant. Since her boobs were in view, I took advantage of the easy access and played with them, raising up her boobs and sucking on the big nipples. She liked that a lot. After a few minutes of that, she cried out.

"Oh, Dirk! I'm so close. It feels so good!"

I kept up the work on her boobs and caressed her ass. She had an idea.

"Put your finger in my ass!"

I wet a finger in the slippery juices around her pussy and reached back for her asshole, sliding my finger in after circling the anus a few times. That pushed her over the edge.

"Mmmmm! Oh! Oh, Dirk! Ahhhhh! Mmmm! Oh, my! Oh, my! Oh, my God! Ahhhhh! I'm coming, Dirk! I'm coming!"

As her body shuddered, I held her by the waist and thrust powerfully upwards into her over and over again, raising her each time I pushed. Her boobs jiggled as I pounded into her, as she closed her eyes and moaned softly.

I came in a torrent of hot cum, spraying her pussy with several jets of the gooey stuff. I relaxed and released her waist, and she opened her eyes and reached for my head, giving me a passionate kiss before sitting back up and smiling.

"I did not even think about coming this morning, that was a nice surprise! Oh, Dirk! What in the hell do you do to me to turn me on like that?"

"It's my charmingly boyish smile and shy personality."

She had a good laugh over that one, which I especially enjoyed with my cock still in her.

"And you really gave it to me good at the end! Man, I thought you were going to launch me off the bed you were pushing me so hard! I loved it!"

I reached up and touched her hair. "I'm glad you liked it. I got kind of caught up in the moment. Are you sore down there?"

She pursed her lips. "My ass is a bit sore, and my vagina is tender, which I guess is to be expected after we've done it about 30 times, most of that pretty vigorously. Jeez, I've lost track of how many times I've come! I know it's more than I ever have." She kissed me. "All because of you, my friend. I'm going to write the Italian sexpot a thank you note!"

"A written statement of my prowess for future relationships will suffice. Applause is always appreciated."

She laughed again. "You are so crazy. Let me get off you and get cleaned up. This girl needs breakfast."

We cleaned up, got dressed, and decided that she should check out of base billeting with me following her, then drive together to an off-base restaurant, and she would leave from there to head home. I took her to an old Shreveport favorite called Strawn's Eat Shop for a down-home breakfast. I usually got breakfast there and took half home for the next day. We were about halfway through breakfast when the waitress came over to refill our coffee.

She smiled and asked us, "How long y'all been dating?"

I looked up in surprise. Meg smiled and answered, "Not long."

The waitress said, "I was watching you from across the room. I can tell by the way y'all are looking at each other."

When the waitress left, I asked, "Is it that obvious?"

Meg laughed. "At this point in our lust filled delirium, a blind man could figure out what we have been doing from 20 paces away."

"Well, we better not be around anyone in your chain of command in that case."

"You've got a point. When you come to see me, I'll not be taking you out to my squadron."

"Speaking of which, get out your calendar, and let's kick around some dates."

We looked at her calendar and decided that a couple of weeks hence would be a nice time for me to come down. After penciling that in and exchanging contact information, there was an awkward pause.

I waited for her to go first. She did.

"Well, Dirk, it's been a crazy fun weekend. I'm so smitten by you that I hope I can concentrate at work until I see you again."

I took her hand across the table. "I'm so glad we met, Meg. This is probably a good time for both of us to remember that we are in the throes of lust right now. I certainly love you as a friend and can't wait until I see you again. But ..."

She interrupted me. "We're not in love, right?"

I smiled. "Right."

She shook her head. "Man, it feels like it right now. My hormones are going freaking crazy. I'll keep telling myself it's just lust. How long does it take for this to wear off?"

"Days, Weeks, months ..."

"Damn. Will seeing each other again make it worse?"

"I think we both know the answer to that."

She thought for a minute. "Let's keep this next visit on the books. Maybe after that, we can calm the hell down and just be occasional ... what will we be?"

"Some people call it friends with benefits. Others call it being fuck buddies."

She laughed. "I think friends with benefits is more dignified."

"Then we are friends with benefits. I so decree it."

She smiled. "FWB. A nice ring." She looked at her watch. "Dirk, I'm sorry, but ..."

"I know. You have a long drive ahead of you. Let's get you on the road."

In the parking lot, we embraced and shared a long kiss, then I put her in her car. She waved as she drove off. I looked back at the restaurant for some reason and saw our waitress looking at me through the window and smiling.

Back at Ronni's, I washed her sheets and remade the bed, wishing to hell that I had paid attention to the arrangement of the multitude of pillows she had on the bed. After picking her up at the airport on time, she chattered about the trip and how it all had gone. We talked about dinner, and she claimed she was starving. I innocently pointed out that there was leftover shrimp creole in the fridge. Ronni looked at me funny.

I said, "I decided to do a little Cajun last night."

She nodded her head and decided to say nothing.

New Orleans and beyond

The intervening two weeks until I saw Meg again passed quickly. I called her at her home a few times for discretion's sake, and we had some great talks. I scheduled my FAA physical for the Tuesday after my trip to New Orleans and hoped that I could pass the Class One exam.

Our reunion was blissful and fun-filled. We danced in the kitchen, cooked together, ate Cajun pot food in the French Quarter, had Hurricanes on Bourbon Street, and had beignets at Café Du Mond. Of course, we had wonderful sex. The visit was over too soon, and the long drive back north was a thoughtful one. Was it time for a long-term relationship?

On Tuesday I passed the physical and was soon in the car heading out to look at a couple of big flight schools on Wednesday. I picked one in Atlanta and started my commercial pilot training right away and moved out there. I got back to Shreveport to work at the simulator a few times but was bleeding cash so badly I couldn't afford another trip to New Orleans, and Meg couldn't get away to Atlanta. We stayed in touch but did not see each other.

About five years later, I got a call from Meg out of the blue. We had kept up with each other's contact information and talked now and then. I had stayed in my condo in Atlanta and was fairly stable as far as that went, but she got several assignments and was moving around. After catching up a bit, she got to the purpose of the call.

"Dirk, how would you like to sleep with a full Colonel?"

I was stunned. "Holy crap, Meg! Did you get promoted?"

She laughed. "Yes, I did and just pinned on my eagles today. I can't stop looking at myself in the mirror."

"That's wonderful! I'm happy for you and proud of you!"

"The offer stands, Mr. Caldwell. How soon can you get to DC and do me?" She was stationed at the Pentagon by then.

I was flying for a regional airline by then and had travel privileges. "Let me look at my schedule, Colonel. I'll see if I can fit you in."

We set a date, and she picked me up at the train station near the suburb where she lived in Virginia. We had a great visit and recreated our special time that we had enjoyed in New Orleans. When that drew to a close, I remarked that she should call me for a visit like this every time she got promoted. She agreed.

As before, we stayed in touch, and I saw her occasionally when I was not dating someone exclusively. She even made it out once to the houseboat I had at the time, and we had great fun.

Then the events of 9/11 happened, I got furloughed and was down in the dumps for a long time. Even talking with Meg could not cheer me up. I didn't see her for years. I just did not want her to see me in such a state.

Eventually, I got recalled back to the airline and things were looking up. After a year or so, I was flying internationally and when I got back from a trip, there was a message from Meg to call her ASAP. I did, and after saying our hellos, she got to the point.

"Mr. Caldwell, how would you like to have sex with a Brigadier General?"

I almost cried; I was so happy for her. "General, I'll see when I can fit you in."

Friday in Dayton

We made a date for me to come to visit her in Dayton, Ohio for a few days where she had taken over a directorate at Wright-Patterson Air Force Base. I arrived on a Friday, and she wanted me to come to her office to meet up. I was picked up at the airport in an Air Force staff car. Since I was a guest of the General, I got VIP treatment. I made sure to dress the part of a successful airline pilot since we would be visiting her at her place of business. I had no idea what to expect.

Meg had an Air Force Captain as her aide, and he made me comfortable in the outer office and got me coffee. We chatted for a while until the General got done with a meeting down the hall. The aide had a few questions.

"Sir, have you known the General long?"

I smiled. "Oh, yes. We're old friends."

He nodded. "You must be special, she had me block out her schedule for the remainder of the afternoon after your meeting."

We were meeting at 2 p.m., so there was still a lot of the business day left. I wondered what she had in mind, maybe a tour?

Around the appointed time, Meg came into the office and greeted me warmly. She was wearing the green camouflage battle dress uniform with cute little combat boots, the single star of her rank on her lapels. She looked great.

"Dirk! So glad you could come. Please, let's go into my office."

The aide followed us in, and she gave him some notes from her meeting and a few tasks to be accomplished. Then she looked at him and said, "Mark this meeting with Mr. Caldwell on the calendar as a private meeting, Jerry. Hold all my calls, and I mean all of them."

He gathered his notes. "Yes, Ma'am. Shall I shut your door?"

She smiled at him and then me. "Yes, please. We'll be reminiscing about old times and would not want to subject anyone to that."

Jerry shut the door quietly on his way out. Meg came to me, stood on her tiptoes, and put her arms around my neck, followed by a deep, passionate kiss. After, she held me tightly and ran her fingers through my hair.

"It's good to see you, Dirk."

I kissed her. "I'm very glad to see you, too."

She moved her arms to encircle my back. "I still have the same spark of excitement when I see you."

"Me, too. I must admit to being a little in awe of kissing a General officer."

She laughed and stepped back. "Well, my devious little mind has been working overtime on how best to capitalize on this occasion."

Oh, boy. "What am I in for?"

She was grinning. She reached into the side pocket of her uniform pants and pulled out a set of black thong panties. I still was not getting it.

"Are you going to model those? Or am I?"

She was still grinning. "No, I stopped in the ladies' room on the way back from my meeting and took these off. Are you beginning to get the idea?"

I was still not getting it. "You'd better spell it out for me."

She came to me and took my face in her hands. "You and I are going to make love right here in my office. You're going to bend me over my desk and do me from behind. You do still like that, don't you?"

To say I was shocked would be an understatement. "Uhhh... yes."

She smiled and started unbuttoning her uniform shirt. "I even wore a bra that has a front clasp to make it easier for you to get to my boobs. We'll leave my pants and boots on, of course."

"Of course."

She came to me and started working on unfastening my pants and belt. "You can take off your blazer if you like."

"Good idea."

She got my pants open and slid her little hand in and made a fist around my cock, which was rising to the occasion.

"Hmm, I think he likes the idea."

"Both he and I do." I started unfastening her pants and reached into them.

I smiled, "Nice. I like the feel of your pubic hair unencumbered by panties."

My hand went deeper, and I slid a finger into her as she gasped. She was wet and warm.

Her gasp changed to a sigh and a light moan. I pushed my finger in deeper and massaged her G spot, right where I remembered it. She moaned and pumped my cock. I may have moaned a little. Things were getting very hot.

Her camouflaged uniform pants fell down to around her ankles. I reached into her open shirt and unfastened the bra, freeing her boobs. I cupped one in my hand and remembered her unique nipples, and then I bent down to take one into my mouth. That caused a small groan. Her pumping of my dick increased, and my pants went to the floor. She raised her mouth to be kissed, so I did that and then, feeling she was ready, I sprang into action.

I grasped her tiny waist and spun her around to face her desk. She braced herself on her elbows and closed her eyes as I put the swollen head of my cock against her labia. She guided me to the hole and reminded me, "Easy on the entry, remember?"

"How could I forget your sweet pussy, Meg?"

I pushed against the resistance of her tight little hole, felt it yield slowly, and then my cock was in her. I pushed all the way in, and she moaned with pleasure. I grasped her tiny ass with both hands and started thrusting into her quickly. We were both caught up in the heat of the moment. I reached around and fondled a boob, squeezing the nipple. She was biting her knuckles to stifle her moaning.

Faster and faster, I pounded into her as her ass pushed back against me with her knees against her desk. She could not help making noise as she got hotter and hotter. I hoped Jerry had the radio on out at his desk. I looked up and saw the blue flag with one star behind her desk signifying her rank, then admired her hourglass waist and cute little ass that I was pounding into. It was a sight, fucking a sexy General officer on her desk during duty hours. Within a few minutes, I felt my balls load up and as I rammed her hard over and over, then I spurted jets of hot cum into her as she raised her head, and her mouth opened with a silent scream of ecstasy. I collapsed onto her back, stroking her boobs and ass as we both panted. She reached across her desk a moment later for a box of tissues and reached behind her to hand me a wad.

I pulled out and wiped my dick off, then put the wad of tissue against her vagina to stem the flood that was about to occur. It would not do for the General to have a wet spot on her crotch walking out of her office after a gentleman had called on her. She put some more tissue on her pussy and then rose and turned around, flushed with excitement.

"Damn! That was fun! I've missed you, Dirk."

I kissed her and started pulling my pants up. She did the same, fastening her bra, buttoning her shirt, and tucking the shirt in. Going to a mirror on the wall, she straightened her hair and put on fresh lipstick. Within a minute, except for her pale skin being flushed, nobody could tell what had just happened. She sat behind her desk and caught her breath, then reached for the phone.

"Jerry, can you have my car brought around? I'm going to take Mr. Caldwell on a tour of the base, then to his quarters after that. No, I'll drive myself."

She hung up the phone and looked at me. "I've got you booked into the distinguished visitor suite."

"Wow, thanks!"

She smiled. "You're booked into the suite, but that doesn't mean you are sleeping there."

I had to smile. "General, do you have plans for me?"

She smiled coyly. "You know me. I'm a planner."

We walked out of the office, and Jerry stood up. "Your car is waiting, Ma'am."

"Thanks, Jerry. Would you call the altitude chamber and the museum for me? I'm going to take Mr. Caldwell to each of those places. They don't need to do anything; it's an informal visit and we'll show ourselves around."

Jerry nodded. "Yes, Ma'am."

She continued. "Then we'll have dinner at the Officer's Club, I'm not sure what time since we will be at the museum looking around."

Jerry nodded again. "I'll call the club and make sure they have a table for you in the private dining room."

She smiled at her aide. "Thanks, Jerry. You're a treasure."

He said, "My pleasure, Ma'am." He turned to me. "Nice to meet you, Mr. Caldwell. Enjoy the base tour."

I shook his hand. "Thanks for all the help, Captain. General Devereaux has told me how much she appreciates you."

Jerry beamed and opened the door to the hallway for us.

As we walked out, Meg said, "You were very kind to Jerry. He's been on pins and needles wondering exactly who you are. All I told him was that you were an airline pilot and old friend who was stopping in to say hello."

She stopped at a ladies' room on the way out, whispering to me, "I need to put panties back on to catch any drips. We'll be out for a while."

We walked outside the building into the beautiful fall afternoon, to a blue Air Force staff car that a young sergeant was standing patiently by. When he saw Meg coming, he went to the front bumper and pulled a cover off a plate that had her one star of rank. He made it to the door and opened it while saluting her. She returned the salute and thanked the sergeant while smiling at him. The kid ran around to the other side of the car and opened the right front door for me. I thanked him. It was the first time in my life that an Air Force member had opened a car door for me. I was traveling in rarified company.

We drove off, with Meg saying, "I thought you'd like to drop by the altitude chamber first. I imagine you went to it when you were stationed in Indiana."

I nodded. Aircrew members attended physiological training every three years, and I had been to this very facility. It was very thoughtful of her to think of that.

"Thanks, MJ. That's nice of you. Hey, we did not talk a lot in your office..." She looked at me, smiling. "I'm not complaining. What are you working on now?"

"I'm the director of a classified project that deals with stealth technology. That's all the public can know."

I laughed. "Good enough for me. I was hoping you would be involved with something cool."

The base was organized into three areas (at the time). We drove from the area where Air Force Systems Command had its buildings off the base and into another section called Area B which was more utilitarian. As we drove and chatted, military personnel on the streets would see the staff car with the star symbolizing a General inside and salute as we went by. We pulled up to the altitude chamber to a parking spot right in front with a sign indicating General officer parking. Jerry had called ahead, and the officer in charge was waiting for us.

As we greeted the officer in charge, Meg made a point of putting him at ease. "You didn't have to go to this trouble. I just want to show Mr. Caldwell the chamber since he attended training here when he was on active duty."

The Lieutenant Colonel was put at ease. "Thanks, Ma'am. When your aide called over to say you were coming to look around, we did not know quite what to expect. Can I show you our facility?"

We had a nice tour, and I enjoyed watching Meg interact with the personnel we came across. They all seemed stunned that this pretty, tiny redhead was a General officer. We left as soon as we could to keep from disrupting their work and headed for the Air Force museum.

The same reserved parking spot was in place at the museum, and a civilian guy in a suit was waiting by the door. Meg went straight up to him and after shaking hands, told him we were just going to look around and did not need any special escort. He left us alone to look around, and we had a quick look around. You can spend days there just looking at exhibits.

Afterward, we went back to the main base, and she took me to the billeting office to sign in for my room. With that done, we went to the Officer's Club for dinner. We were seated in a small, private dining room. When the waiter left with our drink orders, I realized that I had not been in an Air Force club with Meg since the first night we had met. I mentioned it to her.

"Dirk, I've told you that my goal was to be a General Officer. I achieved that. You wanted to be an airline pilot, and you achieved that. I'm now thinking that I will probably not get promoted again, which is fine with me. I can now be a woman first and an officer second, which I have reversed since I graduated from the Academy. If the General has a gentleman caller over to her house, who the hell cares at this point? I want to show you off and take you wherever I want, and to hell with anyone who looks down their nose at that."

I was deeply touched. "I'm tempted to kiss the General here in front of everyone, but decorum stops me from doing so. May I have a raincheck?"

She smiled. "You may. You may also hold the General's hand under the table. Why are we talking about me in the third person?"

We both laughed. Our drinks came, and we enjoyed catching up. I told her about feeling better about myself since I got back to flying. "I was in a dark place for a while, MJ. I had serious doubts about myself."

She nodded. "I tried to get you out of your temporary shell, to cheer you up. I was about ready to drive down to Atlanta and kick your ass, along with the girlfriend that you broke up with."

"You should have. I'm better now."

"What about the girlfriend? Jess, was it?"

I sighed. "I thought she was the one. But it ended badly, and … it's still bad."

Meg touched my hand. "I'm sorry, Dirk."

Our dinner came, and after we finished, the waiter asked if we wanted dessert. Meg said, "No, thanks. I have something at home." She smiled at me mischievously.

We left and got in her staff car. She said simply, "I'm taking you home with me."

Once in her modest base house, she made sure the shades were down, then came to me, again standing on her tiptoes and kissing me deeply as her arms went around my neck and mine wrapped around her.

"Mmmm. I've been wanting to do that all afternoon, even at the altitude chamber and the museum."

"I like kissing Generals. I may make a habit of it."

Another coy smile appeared. "Have you ever had a blow job from a General?"

"I think we both know the answer to that."

She worked on loosening my trousers and kept smiling. "Prepare for a new experience."

"While you are working on that, what's the plan for my visit?"

She looked at me coyly. "I have some fantasies in addition to planning on having sex about a dozen times, in a dozen different ways. Then between sex sessions, I'll take you back to the museum."

I had to laugh as I unbuttoned her uniform shirt. "Only a dozen? Okay, clue me in on your fantasies."

Giggling, she said, "Three of them involve you screwing me while I am wearing my stars."

I was confused. "Three of them?"

"Yes, three. Oral, vaginal, and anal."

I was impressed. "Wow, that's interesting. How will that work?"

She smiled again. "This one will be me blowing you to orgasm while I am wearing only my uniform shirt."

My cock began to get stiffer. "You have interesting fantasies."

She had my pants down by this point and was pumping my cock.

"Let's get naked, except for my shirt."

I started getting serious about getting both of us undressed and soon had a pile of clothes on the couch. She was naked except for her shirt and bra, which was unfastened, exposing her boobs. I was naked all the way, and at her urging, was sitting on her couch.

She knelt before me and took my cock into her small mouth, starting an enthusiastic blow job. Her tongue wrapped around my shaft and circled the glans as her head bobbed up and down as she took me down her throat. It felt fantastic. I reached for her boobs and caressed them, tweaking the nipples as I did so. I put one hand on the back of her head and urged her on. After a few minutes, I felt pressure rising in my balls in response to the eager head job.

I gasped, "Meg! I'm about to come!"

She said with a mouthful of dick, "Stand up!"

I did so, and she wrapped her arms around the back of my thighs, keeping me from pulling away. I looked down at the top of her head and her uniform collar with the stars on her lapels swaying as her head bobbed back and forth with new vigor like a redheaded woodpecker rapidly stroking my cock with her mouth.

It was too much. I came with a loud groan, shooting jets of hot cum into her mouth and down her throat. Spurt after spurt of semen squirted into her mouth as she rolled her tongue around the head, licking off every drop. After my dick started to soften, she drew back and looked up at me in triumph, as if she had accomplished a great task.

"There's one fantasy down! How was that?"

I was incredulous. "Damn, Meg! That was fabulous! Why did you want me to come in your mouth?"

She grinned. "That's what bad girls do, and I wanted to be a bad girl. Now, I'm going to rinse this yucky stuff out of my mouth."

She came back a short time later and kissed me, laughing. "Don't worry, I used mouthwash!"

"I had no doubt. I say again, that was fabulous. I can't wait to see the next set of fantasies."

I noticed she had taken off the green uniform shirt and replaced it with a light blue combination four shirt with her star on the dark blue shoulder boards. The shirt was totally unbuttoned. The effect was heightened by the lack of a bra or any other clothing as her nice boobs and ginger bush were in view.

"You look stunning."

She curled up into me and threw a leg across me.

"I wanted to have sex with you so badly! It's been a while for me, and it just wasn't that satisfying. I know you can make me come in several different ways. This promotion was a great excuse to get my Dirk fix."

I stroked her naked legs and ass. "I'm here to help, old friend."

She smiled into my neck. "You are just what I needed. I feel like a real woman with you."

I moved her around until she was lying with her back to me, her legs off to one side. I had access to lots of nice things. Taking advantage of that, I spread her legs a little, then ran my fingers over her ginger pubic hair, and stroked the labia, which got a groan from her. I then caressed her boobs, working on the big nipples and giving the boobs a good massage. She sighed as I did so, enjoying the attention. Her hips moved gently as I ran my finger up and down her slit. I kissed the side of her head and neck as I did so, with her smiling and moaning softly with her eyes closed.

After about five very sexy minutes of that action, she rose. "Time for dessert!"

"I can hardly wait."

Wearing just the shirt with her badges of rank, she got out one bowl and smiled. "Lovers share dessert according to Gabriella, right?"

"You have an excellent memory."

Into the bowl went a brownie, which she warmed in the microwave. Then she put a scoop of vanilla ice cream on top of the brownie, and drizzled chocolate sauce over both.

I was impressed. "That looks great. Should I put some clothes on?"

"No, I like you naked."

We sat at the corner of the table and shared the dessert in silence. When it was done, she sat back and reached for the chocolate syrup with a grin on her face.

She pulled her shirt apart and dribbled a little of the chocolate on a nipple, recreating a scene from 10 years before at Ronni's house.

"Would you look at that! I've gone and spilled chocolate sauce on myself. What can you do to help, Dirk?"

"I suppose I can help clean it off. Oh, darn! I don't have a napkin. May I lick it off?"

She was grinning. "Oh, that would be so nice of you."

I leaned in and commenced cleaning the nipple with great vigor. It stood up to meet me, and I gave it a thorough cleaning and sucked it, and nibbled a little to make sure it was happy. Then somehow, the other nipple got chocolate on it, so I had to give that one some attention, too. Chocolate-flavored nipples are the best.

Then she dribbled some chocolate on my exposed naked dick, and without urging got on her knees and again took my cock into her mouth, giving it a good cleaning. My cock was stiffening up nicely considering it had a full-scale blow job a short time ago.

I pulled Meg to her feet, then onto my lap, straddling me as I sat in the kitchen chair. My dick was stiff enough to go to work, so I moved the dick to the naked labia. I pushed in a little and felt her tight hole expand slowly, then I was in her. She sat down on my dick and started moving her hips back and forth with me deep inside her, my cock getting stiffer by the second.

She gasped, "Oh, my clit is up against you hard! Oh, it feels so good!"

As she ground her clit against my pubic bone, I felt her reach around for something. She leaned her head back and shot some chocolate into her mouth, then kissed me. That was a great sensation, feeling and tasting the chocolate in her mouth on her tongue as her pussy ground against me. She repeated the chocolate kiss a few times to my delight as our pelvises ground against each other. She was moaning nearly constantly now, and I felt she was nearing an orgasm.

Meg gasped, "Stick your finger up my ass!"

I dipped my finger in some pussy juice for lubrication, then reached around and circled her anus a few times, then inserted it up to the knuckle, and started finger fucking her ass. She moaned loudly and then started to exclaim loudly.

"Mmmmm! Ooohhh! Mmmm! Ahhhhh! Oh, oh, oh! Oh, God! Oh, my! Mmmmm! Oh, Dirk! I'm coming! Ahhhhh!"

She threw her head back and let out a low guttural scream, fully engaged in the orgasm. I felt her body shudder, and she collapsed against me, breathing heavily. I was still stroking into her, working hard to get the third orgasm of the afternoon and evening. I pushed harder into her, and she woke back up and started a fantastic hip motion, rocking her pussy into me.

After a few minutes of frantic activity, I came with a loud groan and shot what sperm I had left into her in several spurts. She collapsed on me again, spent from the activity and still feeling her orgasm fade. I stroked her hair, back, and ass, hoping the neighbors had not heard her scream. I kissed her neck and ears as she recovered slowly.

A few moments later, she raised her head and looked at me with a grin. "Damn, Caldwell! You can still rock my world! That was fucking great!"

"The chocolate kiss was a crowning touch. I loved it!"

She kissed me a few times, then started to get off me, with cum and pussy juice dripping out of her onto my thighs. I reached for a few paper napkins, and we wiped up a little, then she hobbled off to the bathroom with a wad of paper between her legs stemming the flow of juices, still wearing the blue shirt with her badges of rank.

She came out a few minutes later and called, "Shower time!"

I went to the master bath to find her naked, getting the shower warmed up. We enjoyed a lovely shower together like old times, taking turns washing each other's private parts. My cock did not respond to a nice washing, he was fucked out for the night. We enjoyed embracing in a soapy, slippery erotic hug and caressed each other for a while.

Toweling off, she put on shorty pajamas and started getting ready for bed. I had a question. "Am I staying here or going to the DV quarters?"

She smiled, and said, "My gentleman caller is staying the night."

We climbed into bed and snuggled, kissing a few times.

"Hold me while we go to sleep, Dirk."

We fell asleep with me holding my tiny friend. As I dozed off, I smiled as I thought about the events of the day. She was as sexy and fun as ever, and I enjoyed her company.

Saturday morning at the General's quarters

In the morning, we awoke at about the same time and cuddled for a while before each of us made the obligatory bathroom trip. As I got back in bed, she grinned and asked, "Coffee first, or sex first?"

"I can have coffee anytime."

She laughed. "I like the way you think, Caldwell."

I started caressing her on the outside of her pajamas and soon felt her nipples become erect in response to my rubbing of her boobs. I slid a hand into her pajama bottoms and played with her pubic hair and then ran my finger up and down her slit, causing her to moan a little. I then slipped the bottoms off and inserted a finger into the gap between her labia, getting a good moan. She had slipped a hand into my underwear and was playing with my dick. I liked that a lot.

I unbuttoned her top and got better access to her nice boobs, playing with them and kissing them. She put a hand behind my head and ran her fingers through my hair as I did so. I was in no hurry, so I gave her boobs lots of attention as my finger slid deeper into her tight hole and massaged the G spot. Meg showed her appreciation by squirming her hips and groaning some more. After several minutes of this, she had a request.

"Can you give me some head?" she gasped.

I smiled at her and kissed her again. "I thought you'd never ask."

Moving to kneel between her knees, I spread the legs much more than I needed to, making a sexy setting. She lay spread-eagled before me, with an unbuttoned pajama top on, boobs exposed with her big nipples fully erect, her hourglass figure and flat stomach before me as I admired her neatly trimmed ginger pubic hair and her pretty legs. I looked up and saw her green eyes flashing with excitement and a smile on her face. I bent down and took an exploratory taste by sticking my tongue in her. Her eyes closed and her head lolled back as my tongue went deep in her, curving up to taste her G spot.

Then she said, "Wait a minute, I almost forgot!" and wriggled off the bed and dashed to the closet. I was wondering what she was up to as she returned, pulling on her service dress blue uniform coat, complete with ribbons, badges, stars, and nametag. It went on over her naked body, and she climbed back in bed, rummaged around on the bedside table, and held up a couple of cloths and a small tin of Vaseline.

With a grin on her face, she announced, "Fantasy number three will commence shortly!"

I shook my head, smiling. "You are a planner, MJ!"

Meg resumed her place on her back, propped up on a couple of pillows so she could watch. She spread her legs wide and invited me back to her pussy with a smile while pulling her uniform coat open to expose her boobs. This was going to be fun for her, I could tell.

I went back to her pussy and enjoyed the aroma and texture. She smelled wonderful, still having a hint of our soapy wash the night before and the wonderful scent of pussy. I gave her a thorough tonguing, going up to the clit and down into her hole, licking the inside of the lips as I went back and forth. Soon my face was covered in my saliva and her pussy juice, as I gave her the best that I had. She was groaning constantly, squirming her hips and thrusting them into my face. Then she grabbed my head with both hands and pulled me hard into her pussy as she pushed her hips into my face.

She was close to orgasm when she called out, "Do it now, Dirk! Fuck me in the ass! I want to come with your dick in my ass!"

I rolled her over to her hands and knees, and taking the tin of Vaseline from her, rubbed a little on the vaginal hole and some on her asshole. I slipped my cock into her pussy and pushed gently to overcome the resistance while I finger fucked her ass as she groaned and moaned. After a minute of fucking her sweet pussy, I pulled my rock-hard cock out of her pussy and pushed the swollen head against her anal sphincter, easing into the hole, feeling it yielding to steady pressure. I steadily pushed into her ass, feeling it ease as I gently stroked in. She was groaning steadily as I slowly and gently worked my cock until it was all the way in her ass.

She gasped out, "Is it all the way in?"

"Yeah, I'm all the way in."

"Okay, fuck me and play with my boobs and clit! And Happy Birthday!"

"What?"

She laughed as I started fucking her ass. "I'll tell you later!"

I shook my head and started tickling her clit with one hand while squeezing her boob with the other as I went in and out of her ass. Her reaction was immediate, and within a few minutes, the groaning and moaning became constant, then she became vocal.

"Ooooohh! Mmmmm! Oh, wow! Ahhhh! Oh, oh, oh! Owwww!" Then her head rose, and she shouted with ecstasy, "Oh! Oh! I'm coming! Keep it up! Ahhhh! Oh, my God! Oh, my God! Ohhhhh!"

I have always liked screamers, it's validation that I was doing things right. I pumped her ass and tickled her clit while her body shuddered and then her head went down. "Oh, wow. "Oh, wow!" I was still stroking away, feeling like I was getting near my own orgasm.

Her head turned back toward me. "Do it as hard as you want so you can come!"

I took that as permission to crank it up and grasped her by her cute ass and started pounding away. Within a few minutes, my load of cum exploded into her ass, and I exclaimed loudly. As I came, I saw her uniform coat with her General officer star up around her waist, with my hands on that beautiful naked ass with my dick sticking in it as cum started to leak out. It was a wonderful sight. She pushed her ass back into me and gave it a wiggle, which felt great.

I was the first to speak. "That was fantastic, MJ. Are your fantasies now complete?"

She laughed. "Most of them. Now we've done oral, vaginal, and anal with me wearing my rank. That's one of the fantasies. It just felt so naughty, and I wanted to do that with you ever since we had met for sex when I got promoted to Colonel five years ago."

"You are indeed a planner."

I pulled out of her ass and wiped up the drips with a cloth. She put one between her butt cheeks and trotted for the bathroom, all with her uniform coat open and showing her naked ass and legs. It was a sight I'll never forget. There was something about women who achieved high rank in the service that made them want to cut loose and indulge in wild sex. I remembered the night I had with Army Colonel Marylin when I was still in the Air Force. Good times.

Meg came out of the bathroom naked and pulled on a tee shirt. She looked at me and smiled sweetly. "Time for coffee and breakfast."

I pulled on a tee shirt and shorts from my suitcase and joined her in the kitchen. She was humming happily and had coffee going while she puttered around with eggs and some other ingredients. She assigned me toast duty, and in a short while, we were sitting down to omelets, toast, and coffee. I regarded her as we ate.

Her hair was the same shade of red, with a few grey streaks. The pretty green eyes had the start of crow's feet wrinkles, and there were a few more smile lines around her mouth. She still had a spray of freckles across her nose and cheeks. A slight touch of flesh was under her chin and on her neck. I recalled from when I was between her legs that her stomach was still flat, and her gorgeous thin waist still looked like an hourglass. Her ass was firm and her legs lithe and pretty above her tiny little feet with cute painted toes, She was quite a package.

She smiled as I looked at her. "Are you checking me out, Mr. Caldwell?"

"More like admiring you. You look great."

She dimpled and blushed. "Thank you, kind Sir. I think we are both doing well for our age, which is closer to 50 than 40. Do you think my boobs are sagging a little?"

"They and your ass still look magnificent."

She laughed. "You say the sweetest things. After breakfast, we will go by your room and make it look slept in, so the housekeepers won't talk."

"Okay with me. What's the agenda after that?"

"After your room, I thought you'd like to go back by the museum and spend the day there."

"That would be great, but would that interest you?"

She nodded. "Sure. I'm a history buff, and it will be fun walking around with you so you can explain some of the airplane stuff I don't understand too well."

"I'd like nothing better than to walk around the museum with a sexy little redhead on my arm."

She grinned. "And I get to walk around the museum with a tall, sexy airline pilot. It's a win-win. After that, we'll go by the commissary and get some stuff for dinner. I want to cook for you."

"I am totally in agreement with that plan."

We cleaned up the kitchen together and dressed casually for our day. She looked great in tight jeans and a pretty top, with a light jacket for the cool fall weather. She put on tiny little athletic shoes to walk around the museum, and we left for the DV quarters in her personal car with me driving. We were as incognito as we could get, except that there were not too many 4'10" redheads on the base.

Entering the room, I closed the door behind us. She turned to me and stood on her tiptoes for a kiss, which I enjoyed. After a minute, she smiled and said, "Shall we mess up the bed?"

I had to laugh. "Another fantasy, MJ?"

It was her turn to laugh. "No, but it sounds like fun to make out in the DV quarters. Besides, I've been so horny for you I don't think I can get enough of you while you're here!"

I started to relent. I mean, who wouldn't give in to a horny redhead? "Well, maybe just a quickie…"

She started to unfasten her blouse after shedding her jacket. "That's the spirit! You don't even have to make me come; I just want you to fuck me."

I laughed again. "Why MJ! I've never heard you use such language!"

Laughing, she said, "You bring out the woman in me, Caldwell. The horny, slutty woman that is ready to spread her legs and talk dirty to you if that's what it takes."

I was taking off my shirt and dropping my pants. "I'm very appreciative of the enthusiasm."

We pulled the covers back and I knelt between her legs. Since we did not have Vaseline with us, I took on the responsibility of lubricating the vagina with my tongue. After wetting her down and tickling her G spot, she wiggled and moaned. I put my stiff cock against her pussy lips as she spread them wide to make room for the head. I went up against her tight hole and pushed steadily until it gave way. Once in her, I was so enthused by the notion of the quickie that I went to work thrusting hard and fast. I looked into her eyes as she smiled and pushed back at me with her hips.

"Oh, yeah Dirk! Give it to me hard!"

I was getting wound up, so I raised her ankles above my head and drilled her like there was no tomorrow. She groaned and bucked into me, and a few minutes later, I emptied a load of cum into her as I groaned loudly. As I lay on her afterward, she stroked my hair and whispered into my ear, "That's exactly what I wanted. Hard, fast, and sexy."

I smiled at her and kissed her. I got up and got a cloth from the bathroom and we cleaned up. After getting dressed and patting her hair back into place, she smiled.

"That was fun. Now I can say I've done it in the DV quarters."

I had a thought. "What was that about my birthday earlier?"

She grinned. "When we did anal sex the first time, I think I told you I wasn't that crazy about it but would do it for you on your birthday."

I had to laugh. "I sort of remember that."

She kissed me. "I've missed a few, but Happy Birthday."

"My favorite gift, thanks."

We left the DV quarters and headed to the museum. Spending the day there with Meg was awesome. Between the exhibits and being with her made the day special. We held hands a lot and even kissed under some of the exhibits and in the cockpit of one of the planes. It was a special day with a special lady.

We left there and shopped at the commissary like a couple that had a long history of being close. She got items for her famous shrimp creole and dirty rice. My mouth was watering with the thought of the Cajun favorites. We then stopped by the Class Six store for some wine.

Back at her house, she assigned me music duty while she got dinner underway. I found a smooth jazz station, and we slowly danced in the kitchen in our sock feet while dinner simmered. It was a nostalgic return to the several times we had been together.

She asked, "Remember dancing in the kitchen at Ronni's house? And on your houseboat?"

I smiled at the memories. "That was so fun and romantic."

"You are a romantic, Mr. Caldwell. When are you going to make an honest woman out of me?"

I looked at her in surprise. "Two things. First, are you thinking about starting a long-term relationship like marriage? And second, is that an offer?"

She looked wistful. "I think I am ready to settle down now that I made my goal. I like being a General. It doesn't suck. Now I can think about being a woman. What do you think? And by the way, yes that was an offer."

I kissed her as we swayed to the music. "You would be my first choice if I ever do get serious. I just don't think I ever will."

She put her face against my chest. "Not to be argumentative, but you were getting serious with that Jess chick."

I grimaced. "Yeah and look where that got me. Heartbreak Hotel."

She stopped dancing and looked up at me. "I'd never hurt you, Dirk."

I stared into her pretty green eyes for at least 30 seconds, then kissed her again.

I said softly, "No, Megan Juliana, my love. I don't think you would. I'm just not sure I could ever be the man you deserve."

She nodded and looked thoughtful. We went back to dancing, not saying a word. After a minute, the timer went off and she busied herself at the stove while I poured us more wine.

We ate in near silence. She still made a wonderful shrimp creole. After we cleaned up, we curled up on the couch together and quietly watched some comedy shows on TV. Soon it was time for bed.

"Well, there's one more fantasy you can help with."

"I'm all ears."

"They gave us a security briefing at our General officer orientation. We have to be careful when traveling to keep safe from kidnappers. If one of them were to capture me and tie me up ... Who knows what they would do to me?"

My cock was stirring. "Would they tie you up and ... do things to you?"

She grinned. "Exactly."

I pondered this as she came into my arms. "Do you happen to have any rope?"

"No, but maybe some belts might come in handy."

"I have a tie, also. We can make do. When do we start this fantasy?"

"Soon. I'm getting rather worked up just thinking about it. Have you done this kind of thing before?"

I thought of Erika and tried not to smile. "Yes, but only for research purposes."

She laughed. "Caldwell, you are so full of shit. Tie me up and have your way with me!"

"Okay! Do you want some role-playing?"

She thought for a moment. "Sure, why not?"

I nodded. "I'll try some drama, but in case you get uncomfortable, your safe word is, ABORT, ABORT, ABORT and I'll stop and untie you."

She nodded. "Got it."

I pulled her shirt off over her head, then got my belt from my trousers, and got two of hers from her closet, along with a scarf. She watched me with curiosity. I took my belt and wrapped it around her wrists behind her back. Then I used two of her belts and tied her ankles together. She was naked and immobile. I had a spare belt, which I had plans for.

I took her scarf and blindfolded her. She was on her side, bound at hands and ankles, with the blindfold. I kissed her cheek and said, "The simulation is beginning," then left the room.

Hostage situation

I looked at my watch and waited two minutes, which would seem like an eternity if one were bound and blindfolded. I then went to the bedroom door and called out loudly in as foreign as I could make my voice sound.

"So! This is what my freedom fighters have captured! A tiny woman General! Ha, ha, ha!"

Meg jumped as I had called out.

I went to her and took her by the arm.

"What a specimen! A true Yankee imperialist dream. A woman and a General! Ha! You will soon be chained naked to a tree with my goats! I spit on your Yankee beliefs!"

She squirmed in my grasp.

"There must be some mistake..."

"SILENCE! You are my captive, and I am your master! Do not speak unless I tell you to!"

She replied, "I'm an American officer and ..."

"SILENCE!" I swatted her ass with a belt. She jumped.

"I will now humiliate you with the depraved sex acts you have done with your boyfriend. By the way, he will be executed on the cargo ship we will take to the homeland. You will watch him die. Open your mouth and prepare to receive my manhood. If you bite me or fail to please me, I will tie you to a tree spread-eagled for all the village men to defile you! Open your mouth, infidel!"

I pulled her roughly to the side of the bed. She opened her mouth, and I put my half-erect cock into it.

"Pleasure me! Or I will chain you by the neck to a tree!"

She began a blow job, bobbing her head while blindfolded.

"Ah, yes! Bring me pleasure me and you will live!"

My cock got stiffer as she blew me, and I decided to move on after a few minutes.

"Now, prepare to receive me in your female hole. I will service you as you lay on your side since you are bound."

I pulled my dick out of her mouth and spun her around so her ass was facing me, then bent over her as she lay on her side. I spread her legs as much as I could and pushed the head of my cock up against her labia and pushed in, feeling her tight hole give way. Once in, I started a hard humping and fondled her boobs and ass roughly.

"Ah, you are as tight as a virgin. Is it possible you are a virgin? I have had many virgins, and they were similar to you. Ah, your tight hole pleases me. Move your body to give me pleasure, or I will surely beat you."

She started a hip thrusting motion to the side as I fucked her.

"You are an intelligent woman, to give me pleasure. I will have you as often as I wish, you will be my special concubine. You are no longer an officer of the American military; you are my slave. You will tell me of your special classified program, or I will have you beaten and defiled in my village. Do we understand each other?"

She nodded her head as I fucked her.

"Good! Now I will have you pleasure yourself while you pleasure me!"

I scooped her up and carried her over my shoulder into the kitchen. I sat down in the kitchen chair and turned her so she would straddle me, although with her hands and feet bound, she relied on me to keep her upright. I pushed my dick up into her as she groaned with excitement and pleasure.

"Yes! This is good! Give me much pleasure and I will not beat you. Move your body to give me an orgasm! Do it now!"

She now was impaled on my dick and was rocking her hips back and forth, groaning as her clit ground against my pelvis.

"Ah! Good! Make yourself achieve pleasure! Here is something to help you!"

I swatted her ass again with the belt. She jumped and moaned while her hips ground against me. She was getting hot, and so was I.

"Faster! Bring me to orgasm or I will beat you!"

Meg groaned and strained as she rocked her hips into me, pushing mightily against me. She was close to coming. I swatted her ass again.

"Harder! Bring pleasure to my loins, or I shall beat you harder!"

She worked her hips faster, feeling the orgasm begin. I lubricated my index finger in her pussy juices and stuck it up her ass. She groaned and shook in response.

"Ha! I am defiling you and you gain pleasure from this! Infidel! You will make me come to orgasm or you will pay!"

Her body shook in orgasm as she shuddered and moaned. I lifted her and carried her to the couch, where I bent her over the arm. She was helpless, face down into the couch cushions with her hands bound behind her and her ankles tied together as her ass stuck up in the air. I roughly spread her legs, then entered her quickly, and started a fast thrusting motion as she was bent over, taking it from behind.

"This is good! I will keep you as my special concubine! Make me have an orgasm, you cursed infidel!"

She tried to wiggle and push back against me, but being bent over the couch arm, she was nearly immobile. I felt my balls loading up and came with a jet of cum deep into her pussy.

"Ahhh! I impregnate you, infidel! You will bear the spawn of my loins!"

I slowed down and stopped, pulling out of her and patted her on the ass as she lay helpless across the couch.

I picked her up and sat her on the couch, untied her feet, then her hands, and gently removed her blindfold.

"Simulation over. Exercise completed. Report your status."

Her eyes were wide, she grabbed me around the neck with both arms and she started babbling.

"Damn, Dirk! You are really good at that! I was actually getting scared for a while as you got into it. I had an orgasm and then it was amazing as you bent me over the couch! It was rougher than we usually do it, but it was okay in that role-playing scenario. Wow! You even whipped me? I never thought I would be turned on by that, but I was! Do I have marks on my ass?"

I turned her around and looked. "Some red marks, I don't think they will develop bruises."

She rubbed her naked butt. "I hope not. If we get into an accident and I end up in the emergency room trying to explain those marks ..."

I handed her a cloth to catch the drips and bent to kiss her.

Meg trotted off to the bathroom and came back with a tee shirt on, snuggling next to me on the couch. She looked up at me and kissed me.

"Damn! I'm still worked up! We can't go to bed for a while, I'm so excited. Let's watch something funny on TV."

We sat on the couch for a while in each other's arms, then she yawned and said she wanted to go to bed. As we got ready, she asked what my travel plans for Sunday were.

"There is a direct flight to Atlanta about 1300, then another about 1700. I'd like to make the first one and have the other as a backup. If I was at the airport by 1215 it would be fine."

"Okay, let's try for that."

We curled up together and went to sleep almost at once, as I spooned against her tiny body.

Sunday Morning

I awoke just at daybreak and eased out of bed to use the bathroom. She smiled sleepily at me as I got back in bed. I kissed her cheek.

"Go back to sleep. Sorry to have woken you."

She stretched and yawned.

"Mmmm. I slept well after you scared me last night. Let me use the bathroom and then we'll plan our day."

She came back and hopped into bed, putting her arm across me and a leg across mine. I started caressing her boobs through her tee shirt and got a nice smile in return.

"I guess that answers the question of coffee or sex once again."

I smiled back at her as I reached under her shirt. "I like to be consistent in my responses."

Her nipples woke up instantly as I played with them. I ran a finger into her slit and massaged the G spot, which caused a moan and a wiggle.

"Dirk, do this one without a lot of foreplay, I'm formulating a plan."

I took the hint and tickled her labia a little as I reached for the Vaseline and lubed up her vaginal hole as she groaned. She was pumping my dick, which was ready for action. She wanted to get moving.

"C'mon, I want it right now."

"Your wish is my command, my dear."

I rolled her over and eased her legs open. Kneeling between her thighs, I pushed the head of my stiff dick up against her lips and eased in as she help by spreading the labia for me. After a few short strokes, I was all the way in.

She sighed. "That's the way to wake up. How nice. Do me nice and slow, please. It's kind of dreamy like this."

I started a gentle, yet deep thrusting, and her hips moved up to meet me on each push. She closed her eyes and smiled, as I slowly fucked her. I kissed her boobs a little, not wanting to over-stimulate her in her moment. After several long and sexy minutes, she stretched her arms above her head and yawned again while keeping up the motion.

"Okay, I'm awake now. I almost fell asleep again, which was very nice. Now you may pound away on me like the horny man that you are."

"You know me so well." I picked up the pace and started pushing harder.

She ran her fingers through my hair. "After 10 years or so, I am starting to get to know you. Hurry up and come, I want coffee."

"Be nice, or I'll carry you out to the kitchen impaled on my dick."

She laughed. "You wouldn't!"

"Oh, yeah? Watch this! Cross your ankles behind my back."

She did so and moaned. "I love that."

With her legs up, I maneuvered us to the edge of the bed, and sitting up with her on my lap, I kissed her, then leaned forward to get my center of gravity over my knees, then stood up with her ass in my hands as she squealed.

"Dirk! What the hell?"

I then held her up and walked to the kitchen with her clinging to me with her arms around my neck while gripping me with her legs. She was laughing as I got her out to the kitchen counter and set her ass down.

"Damn, you are crazy, Caldwell! This countertop is cold on my butt!"

I stroked away and she quit complaining. She kissed me hard as I pounded into her and she kept us connected with her legs around my back. I came soon afterward and groaned loudly. She took my head in her hands and stared into my eyes.

"I love you, you crazy ass!"

"I love you, too. See? I have come and you are in the kitchen, ready to make coffee."

She shook her head. "So crazy. Did you hurt your back?"

"Naah. You're just a little bitty person. No strain at all."

"Put me down and give me a paper towel. Someone made a mess inside me."

I lifted her down and handed her the towel, which she put to use stemming the flow. Afterward, she started the coffee as I watched attentively.

"Barefoot and naked in the kitchen, making the coffee. That's a nice image."

She glared at me. "With your cum running down my thighs, very sexy."

"It is a Kodak moment."

She punched me in the shoulder and stalked off, laughing.

Later, we enjoyed coffee and the Sunday paper at the kitchen table, wearing tee shirts and underwear. She finished a section of the paper and we traded. She stopped what she was doing and took my hand.

"I said I love you, Dirk. It just came out."

I looked into those pretty green eyes. "I love you too, Megan. I have for a long time."

"But we are not going to get into the whole marriage and settling down thing, right?"

I shook my head. "Like I said, I can't be the man you deserve. I'm too scared of commitment and it wouldn't be fair to you."

She smiled. "I get it. The offer is still open if you change your mind."

I reached up to touch her cheek, and her hand held mine there for a moment.

"Thanks, MJ. You're one hell of a woman."

We sat quietly for a while, then she announced the plan for the day.

"We'll have sex once more, shower, and clean up. Then I will take you to the Officer's Club for Sunday brunch on our way to the airport where you will romantically kiss me goodbye in public and fly off into the sunset. How's that?"

"Good, except I am flying south, not west into the sunset."

"Really? That's what you got out of that?"

"Hey, I heard the rest!"

She shook her head in disgust and stood.

"Come on, you ungrateful thing. You have a woman to bring to orgasm, or you ain't getting brunch."

"Now that's motivation!"

We went into the bedroom, stripped off our shirts and underwear, and hopped back into bed. She had a thought.

"I suppose I better rinse out the objective area since I am expecting some great head."

"Good idea. Can I help?"

She smiled. "Hmm. There is an image. Yes."

We had fun rinsing her pussy clean, which was foreplay by itself. After I dried it off, I lifted her onto the bathroom sink and started some preliminary fingering and licking while she moaned appreciatively. Moving to the bed, I sat her up on a couple of pillows and went down on her using everything I had. She groaned, moaned, and squirmed as my tongue went through its paces on her G spot and clit while I massaged her boobs and played with the big nipples.

She was soon begging me to fuck her, so I moved her down and slipped my meat into her. She groaned with pleasure and lifted her knees so I could get deeper. After several minutes of heavy fucking, she wanted to get on top. I thought that was a great idea, she came more easily on top. I rolled onto my back, and she left the bed for a minute and came back. She handed me a belt. I just looked at her.

She blushed, then said, "Use it on my ass when I am getting ready to come. I've already got a few red marks, might as well add a few."

I shrugged. "You got it, MJ." She was getting kinky on me after all this time.

Meg mounted me and slid my stiff cock into her pussy, riding it all the way to the hilt. She gasped as she ground her clit against me and started a rapid back and forth movement. I pushed up into her, meeting her on every push. Within a few minutes, we were breathing heavily with exertion, and she said she was getting close.

"Oh! Oh! Dirk, I'm close. Whip me!"

I took the belt and gave her a good swat on the ass. She jumped and groaned heavily as she kept the frantic hip motion up. A minute later, she wanted it again.

"Again, Dirk! Whip me again!"

I popped her with the belt again, and she threw her head back and let loose with a howl of ecstasy. Then she wanted more.

"Ahhhhh! Shit! Fuck! Again, Dirk! Once more, hard this time!"

I smacked her again, and the crack of the leather belt striking her ass filled the room. She shrieked in delight and pain, then shuddered as the orgasm hit her. Her body quivered and shook, then she collapsed onto me as I shot my load deep in her.

She lay on top of me, panting for several minutes. I stroked her back, trying to stay away from her cute ass, which I was sure had welts from the belt rising up in angry red streaks.

She finally rose, kissed me, then sat up with my dick still in her. She shook herself.

"Wow! You really know how to show a girl a good time, Caldwell. That was fucking incredible!"

"I'm glad you liked it. How's your butt?"

"Oh, it's sore and it's going to hurt to sit down for a few days. You did just what I asked for, please don't have any regrets. I wanted it and you gave it to me. I wouldn't ever let anyone but you do that. I trust you. Damn, you got me started on anal sex, now the belt... what's next?"

"I shudder to think. Let me know."

She laughed and climbed off me, trying to keep the dripping cum and pussy juice under control.

"Oh, jeez. We have fun but make a mess. Come on, wash my back in the shower."

We had a nice shower, and I turned her around to look at her ass. Sure enough, there was one bright red welt and a couple more red marks. I felt kind of bad about it and told her so. She laughed it off and turned around and washed my cock lovingly. My dick liked the attention and stiffened up unexpectedly. She looked at me in amazement.

"Damn, Dirk! Didn't you just come? Did I dream that? You are some kind of stud this weekend."

I shrugged. "I have no explanation except that I'm inspired by your cute, tiny little sexy body."

She laughed again, turned around, and bent over at the waist, bracing herself.

"Have at it, big boy! I can't take you to the club with a raging hard on. What would people think about the kind of host I am?"

I slipped my stiff dick into her nice clean pussy. "You're too good to me."

I started a nice, steady thrusting trying not to push into the welts on her cute little ass. She yelped once as I pushed on one by mistake, I knew she must be sore. It felt great, and the visual image of her tiny body taking my dick in from behind was a real turn-on. This was so much fun, that I almost regretted coming, but I did in a few minutes, groaning loudly. I pulled out and stood there breathing hard. She turned to me and kissed me.

"Now listen, Caldwell. That's the last time for you this trip. If you get another boner, you have to take care of it yourself."

"Got it. Even in the Officer's Club?"

She laughed so hard I thought she would pee herself.

"Yes! Even there."

We cleaned up and got dressed, with her fixing her hair and makeup because there was no telling who we would run into at the club. I got back into my traveling airline pilot outfit of a long-sleeved shirt, slacks, and blazer. She came out in a nice pantsuit looking like the executive she was. I admired her for a moment.

"You are one pretty damned fine looking redhead, MJ."

She dimpled. "Thanks, Mr. Caldwell. You clean up pretty well yourself. Shall we go?"

I drove us to the club in her personal car with her giving directions. The brunch was well attended, and after getting our coffee, we were getting ready to go through the buffet line when a distinguished looking older couple approached us.

The man greeted us, "Hello Meg! How are you?"

She shook hands and said, "Hello, Sir. This is Mr. Caldwell, visiting from Atlanta."

I figured if she called this guy sir, he must be high up on the food chain. "Hello, General. Dirk Caldwell. Nice to meet you." We shook hands and he introduced his spouse.

"Hello, Dirk. Nice to meet you as well. Just here for the weekend?"

I smiled. "Meg has been showing me around this weekend, but I have to get back to Atlanta and work."

He smiled. "I'm glad you had a good tour guide. Enjoy your brunch."

As they walked away, Meg leaned over and whispered. "He's the four-star General commanding Aeronautical Systems Command."

"And now he knows we spent the weekend together. Will that cause trouble?"

She smiled. "Nope. I'm concentrating on being a woman now. If I have a gentleman friend in from out of town, at least I'm not causing a scandal by sleeping with a local."

"Good point."

We sat down and enjoyed the great brunch. Meg winced as she sat down. I looked at her in sympathy. She leaned over and whispered,

"That's the price of having a great experience. I'm not regretting it one bit."

After we ate, we had time for one more cup of coffee before we hit the road. I looked at her.

"Is it okay to hold your hand and gaze into your eyes?"

She smiled. "I thought you would never ask."

We stopped by the billeting office and checked me out of the room I did not use, then headed to the airport on Highway 4, then I-75 to I-70. After a half-hour drive, I pulled up at the terminal and stopped in front of a sign for my airline. I put the car in park and looked at Meg.

"Well, here we are."

She smiled. "Yes, here we are."

After looking into each other's eyes for a moment, she opened her door and got out. I did likewise and met her at the trunk, where I pulled out my battered roll-aboard suitcase. She stood on her tiptoes one more time and with her arms around my neck, gave me a deeply passionate kiss. I looked into her eyes, and we smiled at each other.

"Until next time, Megan Juliana."

"Until next time, Dirk. Remember my offer is still open."

I hugged her tightly. "I will."

I pulled my suitcase over the curb and headed for the door, then looked back. She was still standing there looking my way and blew me a kiss. I blew her one back, then stepped into the terminal and started the trip back to Atlanta and home, wondering if I did the right thing by not accepting her offer of marriage and stability.

A year passed, and I took an upgrade to captain at the airline, then one day ran into Jess on a flight. We reunited and committed to an exclusive relationship that endured.

I did not see Megan again, although we always traded Christmas cards. She always signed, "Your FWB."

Don't miss out!

Visit the website below and you can sign up to receive emails whenever Dirk Caldwell publishes a new book. There's no charge and no obligation.

https://books2read.com/r/B-A-UHDZ-CPMPC

BOOKS 2 READ

Connecting independent readers to independent writers.

Did you love *Redheads need Love: Megan from New Orleans*? Then you should read *Flight Attendants want Love: Flying High with Jessica*[1] by Dirk Caldwell!

[2]

This sizzling novel is an account of a long term relationship. Dirk's stories are told from a man's perspective and point of view. Both men and women will enjoy this book, as the author always weaves a romantic story into the steamy descriptions. I'm sure you will enjoy this book with plentiful details about airline crew romances mixed in with the sex scenes.

Airline pilot Dirk meets flight attendant Jessica, and their initial sexy encounter grows into a relationship that spans decades, through good times and bad. The author incorporates exquisite details, bringing

---

1. https://books2read.com/u/brBaPW

2. https://books2read.com/u/brBaPW

the reader into the bedroom with the couple to feel the heat. Fly along with Dirk and Jessica as they travel the world of sensuality.

Also by Dirk Caldwell

Adventures of Stan
Stan does a Big Girl and gives her a Big Orgasm
Stan Does a Female Police Officer While On Duty
Stan Scores on a Booty Call with Barbara
Stan Takes Barb's Anal Cherry
Stan Teaches Oklahoma Karen About Sex in the City
Stan gets Kinky with Barb on Vacation
Barb Wants more Orgasms with Stan before She gets Engaged to
Another Man
Stan Does Barbara's Mom!

Dirk Caldwell Romantic Erotic Novels
A Visit to the Farm with Darla - a Sexy Short Story
A Layover in Omaha with Tina
A Night in Eufaula with Lynn
A Trip to the Lake with Kim
Older Women need Love, too! Erika visits Atlanta
Lessons in Love: Gabriella visits Indianapolis
Big Girls Need Love, too! Barbara from Kokomo
Flight Attendants want Love: Flying High with Jessica
Back to the Farm with Darla - A Sexy Sequel
Redheads need Love: Megan from New Orleans

A Big Girl finds Love: Joann from Shreveport
Lust from London: My Affair with a British Nymphomaniac
Paula's Sexy European Weekend
Mother and Daughter Threesome

Dirk Caldwell Sexy Short Stories
To All the Girls I've Loved Before: Sexy Short Stories Book 1
To All the Girls I've Loved Before: Sexy Short Stories Book 2
To All the Girls I've Loved Before: Sexy Short Stories Book 3

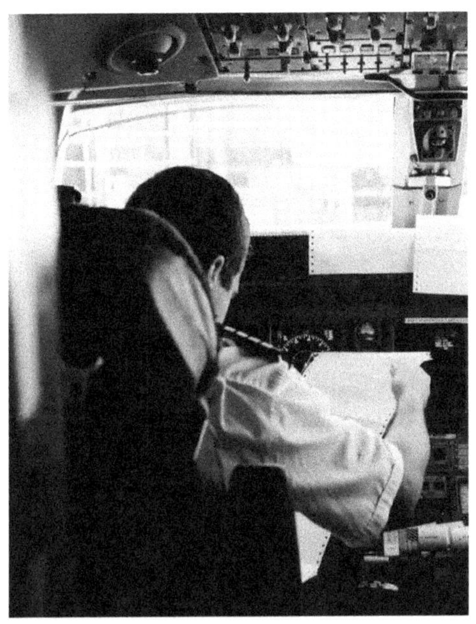

About the Author

Dirk Caldwell is the pen name of the author of an erotic book series. Dirk embodies the life experiences of the author as an Air Force veteran and commercial airline pilot. Most of the content is true and relates to the author's experiences. It's up to the reader to decide what is fiction and what is true life.